PASÓ POR AQUÍ AND *THE DESIRE OF THE MOTH*

PASÓ POR AQUÍ AND THE DESIRE OF THE MOTH

TWO CLASSIC NOVELS OF NEW MEXICO

EUGENE MANLOVE RHODES

INTRODUCTION AND NOTES BY GARY SCHARNHORST

UNIVERSITY OF NEW MEXICO PRESS | ALBUQUERQUE

Pasó por Aquí by Eugene Manlove Rhodes originally published 1926
The Desire of the Moth by Eugene Manlove Rhodes originally published 1916
University of New Mexico Press edition published 2026

Printed in the United States of America

Library of Congress Cataloging-in-Publication Data
ISBN 978-0-8263-6957-4 (paper)
ISBN 978-0-8263-6958-1 (ePub)

Library of Congress Control Number: 2026932209

Founded in 1889, the University of New Mexico sits on the traditional homelands of the Pueblo of Sandia. The original peoples of New Mexico—Pueblo, Navajo, and Apache—since time immemorial have deep connections to the land and have made significant contributions to the broader community statewide. We honor the land itself and those who remain stewards of this land throughout the generations and also acknowledge our committed relationship to Indigenous peoples. We gratefully recognize our history.

Cover illustration by Felicia Cedillos
Designed by Felicia Cedillos
Composed in Adobe Garamond Pro

CONTENTS

INTRODUCTION

EUGENE MANLOVE RHODES (1869–1934) may be the most significant American author lost today in a bibliographical blind spot. A consummate writer of Western fiction, Rhodes was championed during his career by such distinguished Western historians as Bernard DeVoto, J. Frank Dobie, and Walter Prescott Webb. DeVoto declared that Rhodes penned "the finest [novels] ever written about that strange and violent and beautiful era in American life, the years of the cattle trade," indeed the "only body of fiction devoted to the cattle kingdom which is both true to it and written by an artist in prose."[1] According to Dobie, Rhodes was "blood brother" to Mark Twain[2] and authored "a half dozen novels far superior to the false, feeble, and flatulent 'westerns'" of Zane Grey, Max Brand, and their ilk.[3] On his part, Webb believed that Rhodes failed to win wider recognition because "he made his stories true to life in the cattle country rather than to the Eastern notions of what the life there ought to be."[4] No less an author-

1 DeVoto, "Eugene Manlove Rhodes," *El Paso Times*, December 31, 1933, 12; and "The Novelist of the Cattle Kingdom," introduction to *The Hired Man on Horseback: My Story of Eugene Manlove Rhodes* by May Davison Rhodes (Boston: Houghton Mifflin, 1938), xxxix.

2 Dobie, "A Tribute to Gene Rhodes," introduction to *Best Novels and Stories by Eugene Manlove Rhodes*, ed. Frank V. Dearing (Boston: Houghton Mifflin, 1949), xix.

3 "An Appreciation of Professor Dobie," *El Paso Times*, March 15, 1931, 4.

4 Webb, *The Great Plains* (Boston: Ginn, 1931), 463–64.

ity than the Western novelist and historian Walter Van Tilburg Clark considered Rhodes "the peer of Owen Wister in portraying the cowboy in his code" and often "the equal of such factual narrators as Andy Adams and Will James in presenting the mode of his working life. In variety and scope he is the best of the four."[5] Or as Rhodes attested in his own voice, "I can be as modest as anyone where there is anything to be modest about. I will now state clearly that, as far as New Mexico is concerned, the only stories which should sell better than mine, on *account* of *authentic Southwestern flavor*, are these, as follows: None."[6]

He was, after all, a real-life cowboy, rancher, miner, and army scout for twenty-five years. In 1881 he moved at the tender age of twelve with his family to the Southwest and he became a ranch hand a year later. As a teenager he worked for the Bar Cross, a huge cattle operation that stretched a hundred miles by fifty miles across the southern New Mexico desert from the San Andrés mountains to the Rio Grande. He became an accomplished bronco buster, though he spent more time while on horseback reading than roping. He later observed that his fellow cowpokes "were made of watch-springs, whalebone, and dynamite."[7] The genuine wrangler, unlike the caricature portrayed in popular Western fiction and film, "was not a murderer, thief, drunkard, gambler, wastrel, or weakling—but a man who would rank as good as any time or at any place."[8] Most of the men "who carried bad names were as mild-mannered and meek as Sunday school boys."[9] To be sure, he was familiar with criminals in the Territory,

5 Clark, "Chronicler of Cowboys," *New York Times Book Review*, November 20, 1949, 7.

6 W. H. Hutchinson, *A Bar Cross Man: The Life and Personal Writings of Eugene Manlove Rhodes* (Norman: University of Oklahoma Press, 1956), 244. See also George Wharton James, *New Mexico, the Land of the Delight Makers* (Boston: Page, 1920), 365.

7 Katharine Fullerton Gerould, "The Aristocratic West," *Harper's Monthly* 151 (September 1925), 472.

8 Retta Badger, "'Gene' Rhodes: Cowboy and Author," *Los Angeles Times*, July 12, 1931, 112.

9 "Writer Allowed to Carry Gun Without Shells," *Albuquerque Journal*, December 5, 1928, 5.

including "Black Jack" Ketchum, Bill Doolin, and Frank Jackson, because, he explained, "outlaws are more interesting than in-laws. And they are better housemates."[10] But he never celebrated in his fiction the "*men within my knowledge* whose lives were disgusting and shameful."[11] Rhodes numbered among his friends Pat Garrett (1850–1908), the legendary New Mexico lawman who killed Billy the Kid and served at different times as sheriff of Lincoln and Doña Ana Counties; humorist Will Rogers (1879–1935);[12] movie star cowboy Harry Carey (1878–1947);[13] feminist Charlotte Perkins Gilman (1860–1935); artist Charlie Russell (1864–1926); and US Secretary of the Interior Albert Fall (1861–1944), who for his part in the Teapot Dome scandal during the Harding administration was the first Cabinet member in history sent to prison.

Many of Rhodes' characters are extremely well read—he even claimed that cowboys were the most literate class in America.[14] They routinely quote the Bible and the works of such highbrow writers as Keats, Kipling, Robert Browning, Omar Khayyam, and Shakespeare. (For the record, Wister's cowboy hero the Virginian also discusses Shakespeare, specifically *Henry IV, Part I* and *Henry V*, with the eastern schoolmarm Molly Stark Wood.) Lewis D. Fort once observed that his friend Rhodes "had one of the most remarkable memories of anyone I have ever known. One could repeat to him a line or two from almost any of Shakespeare's plays,

10 Hutchinson, *A Bar Cross Man*, 51.

11 Hutchinson, *A Bar Cross Man*, 268.

12 Rhodes once accompanied Rogers and Charles Lummis on a visit to Mission San Juan Capistrano, a holiday Lummis celebrated in a poem titled "The Four Horsemen of the Eucalypts," which includes the lines: "Gene Rhodes whose Southwest stories lope / A gait no other seems to hit" (Turbesé Fiske and Keith Lummis, *Charles F. Lummis: The Man and His West* [Norman: University of Oklahoma Press, 1975], 161). This biography of Lummis also reprints a photograph of Lummis, Rhodes, and Rogers together (162).

13 Carey praised Pringle's character in several movies as "my kind of man. I mean the kind of 'Outwester' I like to play. He smells of greasewood smoke and Bull Durham instead of tan-bark and billposting paste" (Hutchinson, *A Bar Cross Man*, 149).

14 Lee Shipley, "Lee Side o' L.A.," *Los Angeles Times*, November 10, 1928, 20.

and he could not only quote the lines which followed, but he could go on repeating the text for several succeeding pages."[15] More than one critic complained, in fact, that Rhodes' rustic westerners say "things only a Harvard graduate could say."[16] In self-defense Rhodes explained in his novel *Bransford in Arcadia* that "cowboys all smoked" and the Bull Durham Company "placed in each package" of its tobacco a coupon redeemable for a paperback book. "There were three hundred and three volumes on that list" and "each one was a classic. . . . In due course of time they read those books. Some were slow to take to it; but when you stay at lonely ranches" with plenty of leisure time "you must do something. The books were read. Then, having acquired the habit, they bought more books."[17] As a result, DeVoto averred, Rhodes put "much the best dialogue" into the mouths "of Western characters since Mark Twain"[18]—this testimony by the curator of the Mark Twain Papers and author of *Mark Twain's America* (1932).

Incidentally, in the same novel Rhodes coined the phrase "land of enchantment,"[19] which became the New Mexico state motto in 1989, inspired a ballad by Michael Martin Murphey, and today is embossed on official state documents from letterhead to license plates.

More to the point, Rhodes' heroes observe a strict code of behavior. They are invariably good men who adhere to principles of equality (not exactly laws) foreign to many city folk. "I claim for these men of whom I write no greater equipment" than "a joyous and a loving heart, a decent respect for others and for himself, and courage enough to master fear," Rhodes insisted in the preface to his novel *The Trusty Knaves.*[20] His Western *preux chevalier* or *cowboy idéal* was John Wesley Pringle, a recurring

15 Fort, "Poet on Horseback," *This is New Mexico*, ed. George Fitzpatrick (Santa Fe: Rydal, 1948), 74.

16 Shipley, "Lee Side o' L.A.," *Los Angeles Times*, May 17, 1931, 18.

17 Rhodes, *Bransford in Arcadia* (New York: Holt, 1914), 65–66.

18 DeVoto, "The Novelist of the Cattle Kingdom," xlii.

19 Rhodes, *The Trusty Knaves* (1931; rpt. Norman: University of Oklahoma Press, 1971), xxii–xxiii.

20 Rhodes, "A Touch of Nature," *Out West* 29 (July 1908), 73.

character in his fiction named for the Protestant reformer and founder of the Methodist Church, who spurned the Calvinist doctrines of reprobation and innate depravity and affirmed instead doctrines of free will and human perfectibility. Pringle divided all people, as in Christ's parable, into goats and sheep: "One side was scoundrels, traitors, bigots and hypocrites" and corrupt bankers, politicians, merchants, lawyers, and especially politicians beholden to the "Santa Fe Gang" who governed the New Mexico Territory at the turn of the twentieth century. Pringle's (and Rhodes') loyalties lay with "t'other" kind: "Heroes, Patriots, Martyrs and Reformers."[21] Indeed, Rhodes modeled Pringle on his father Hinman Rhodes (1827–1907),[22] a former Union Army colonel, government agent of the Mescalero Apache Indian Reservation from 1889 until 1891, and a devout Methodist. Eugene Rhodes' formal education was mostly limited to two years at the College (now University) of the Pacific, a Methodist school in Stockton, California.

Not surprisingly, he was extraordinarily progressive on issues of race and ethnicity. In 1917, for example, he lauded Diego Dionisio de Peñalosa Briceño y Berdugo, the seventeenth-century governor of Spanish New Mexico, for defending Native Americans during the Inquisition and becoming the first person "in America to strike a blow for freedom."[23] In 1921 Rhodes praised his friend Francisco Bojórquez (1865–1920), twice-elected sheriff of Sierra County and "the best bronc rider and roper in the country," for "common sense" amounting "to genius." He excoriated racist fiction: "The Mexican in our novels is a man of straw: not only a scoundrel, but a stupid and feckless scoundrel, sure to be outwitted, outfought, and 'foiled' by any blond in the book. . . . The people who write this bosh know nothing about Mexicans."[24] In *Pasó por Aquí* ("he passed by here")—Rhodes' masterpiece,[25] according to DeVoto—he favorably portrayed a

---

21 Hutchinson, *A Bar Cross Man*, 285.

22 Rhodes, *West is West* (New York: Fly, 1917), 110.

23 Badger, 112.

24 "Fiction of Mexican Villain Exploded by Eugene M. Rhodes," *New York Tribune*, July 3, 1921, 5.

25 DeVoto, "The Novelist of the Cattle Kingdom," xxxix. The Spanish conquistadors carved these words and hundreds of visitors their names in the soft

fictional Native police chief, Nueces River, and a real former Doña Ana deputy sheriff, Anastacio Barela (d. 1897). As Sanford Marovitz concludes, Rhodes "ennobles" the people of New Mexico in the novel by highlighting "their kindliness and courtesy rather than the malicious, vulgar" stereotypes.[26]

Rhodes' novels *Pasó por Aquí* (1926) and *The Desire of the Moth* (1916), both originally serialized in the *Saturday Evening Post*, are set mostly in the Jornada del Muerto ("journey of the dead") in southern New Mexico, a region stretching between the San Andrés mountain range and the Rio Grande or from the ghost town of San Marcial in Socorro County to the orchards around La Mesilla and the suburbs of Las Cruces. Rhodes' most elaborate description of the territory appears in his novella "Stepsons of Light":

> The Jornada is a high desert of tableland, east of the Rio Grande. In design it is strikingly like a billiard table; forty-five miles by ninety, with mountain ranges for rail at east and west, broken highlands on the south, a lava bed on the north. At the middle of each rail and at each corner, for pockets, there is a mountain passway and water; there are peaks and landmarks for each diamond on the rail; for the center and for each spot there is a railroad station and water—Lava, Engle and Upham. Roughly speaking there is road or trail from each spot to each pocket, each spot to each spot, each pocket to every other pocket.[27]

---

limestone of Inscription Rock in west-central New Mexico.

26 Marovitz, "Eugene Manlove Rhodes," in *Twentieth Century Western Writers*, 3rd series, ed. Richard H. Cracroft (Detroit: Gale, 2002), 258. Put another way, Rhodes portrayed New Mexicans as "rounded" or three-dimensional, realistic characters rather than "flat" or two-dimensional stereotypes. Despite Monte's tortured dialect, he is not a comic character.

27 Rhodes, "Stepsons of Light," *Saturday Evening Post*, September 25, 1920, 132.

In the center of the table, "where you put the pin at pin pool," stood Engle, a thriving regional commercial center at the turn of the twentieth century, today a ghost town a few miles east of Elephant Butte Lake. In all, Rhodes' circumscribed "little world" encompassed the towns of Deming, Silver City, Carrizozo, Alamogordo, Ruidoso, Tularosa, Socorro, and Hot Springs (a.k.a. Truth or Consequences since 1950) as well as White Sands National Park, Oliver Lee Memorial State Park, the Bosque del Apache National Wildlife Refuge, and historic Fort Stanton.

Despite the similarities in setting, the two stories are remarkably different narratives. In *Pasó*, a bank robber named Ross McEwen is pursued by Pat Garrett, one of the honorable officers of the law in Rhodes' fiction. At great personal risk McEwen nurses a Mexican family afflicted with diphtheria back to health and Garrett forgives his bank theft—an action that, as DeVoto suggests, represents something "more profound" about the Western ethos than the lex talionis.[28] McEwen, the outlaw-hero, is nothing less than a type of benevolent angel sent by "the mercy of God" to help the "family," as Garrett recognizes. Or as Eddy Orcutt asserts, "*Pasó por Aquí* is the summary of [Rhodes'] credo" and he not only "assigned a robber and gunman to enact" it, but a Mexican gambler to express it.[29] In *Desire*, an innocent man persecuted by his political enemies and falsely accused of murder is chased by a lynch mob comprised of "simpletons and fools" led by a corrupt sheriff.[30] Both stories recount the adventures of a hero on the lam. Though legal authority is represented in dramatically different ways in the two tales, justice—even if it's vigilante justice—prevails in both cases.

Rhodes "often transmuted real people" into characters in his stories,[31]

---

28 DeVoto, "The Novelist of the Cattle Kingdom," xxxv.

29 Orcutt, "Passed by Here: A Memorial to Gene Rhodes," *Saturday Evening Post*, August 20, 1938, 50–51. Rhodes was a seasoned poker player.

30 Christopher (Chris or Christ) Foy (the archaic French term "foi" or "faith") is persecuted and targeted for martyrdom. His characterization anticipates Rhodes' references to other biblical types in the novel (e.g., Judas and Ananias).

31 Dobie, "Gene Rhodes," xvi. As Rhodes conceded, "In any month in Santa Fe, you may see nearly half the characters of my books walking the streets in flesh and

as Dobie notes, and Garrett's appearance in *Pasó* epitomizes this technique. In 1927, the year following its serialization, Rhodes confessed he had "been irritated for forty years, plus, by the lies told about Pat Garrett." He and Garrett had not always been "friends. For several years, while he was Sheriff of Dona Aña County, I was a torn in his side. . . . But later we became friends—and he was one of Plutarch's men."[32] Rhodes also published a piece, "In Defense of Pat Garrett," in which he vindicates Garrett "from the malignant stupidity which, all his life long, gave him curses when he should have had honor" and "from a hate that will not let him rest in his grave."[33] In addition to Garrett, over a dozen actual New Mexicans make at least cameo appearances in these two tales, including several of Garrett's deputies and ranchers and ranch hands Rhodes knew from his own days on the range.

Rhodes loosely based the initial chapters of *Pasó por Aquí* on an actual bank robbery in Belen, New Mexico, thirty miles south of Albuquerque, in January 1904. Though the bandits were pursued for days, they made a clean getaway through the San Andrés mountains and the alkali flats of southern New Mexico.[34] Ironically, according to his widow May Davison

---

blood. (Penitentiary and legislature located here.) In Albuquerque, Las Cruces and El Paso, you can meet nearly all the other half" (Hutchinson, *A Bar Cross Man*, 245).

32 Hutchinson, *A Bar Cross Man*, 267, 262.

33 Rhodes, "In Defense of Pat Garrett," *Sunset* 59 (September 1927), 26–27, 85–88, 90–91; rpt. *The Rhodes Reader: Stories of Virgins, Villains, and Varmints*, ed. W. H. Hutchinson (Norman: University of Oklahoma Press, 1957), 305–16

34 "Bank Held Up at Belen," *Santa Fe New Mexican*, January 15, 1904, 1. As in Rhodes' novel, the posse trailing the robber(s) comes across one of the horses ridden in the escape: "The Only Trace of Belen Robbers an Abandoned Horse," *Albuquerque Journal*, January 18, 1904, 5. See also "Trip to Rhodes Grave Sunday," *Alamogordo News*, April 16, 1953, 1; "Southern New Mexico Men Characters in New Magazine Story," *Albuquerque Journal*, February 1, 1926, 3. Rhodes based his story "Trail's End," in *Cosmopolitan* for February 1929, three years after the publication of *Pasó por Aquí*, on a bank robbery in Las Cruces in 1900 ("Las Cruces Bank Robbed," *Albuquerque Tribune*, February 14, 1900, 3). The thieves in this case were pursued by a posse led by Garrett and were eventually captured in Texas by one of Garrett's deputies. A brief story about the holdup appeared in the

Rhodes half a century later, her husband was a fleeting suspect in the theft and "got such a kick out of the fact" that he "wrote the story from that inspiration."[35] Eugene Rhodes, too, remembered he was once followed by a deputy sheriff for "nearly four hundred miles" across southern New Mexico, "just behind me but never quite catching up." He had no idea at the time "what [the deputy] wanted me for. There were so many things."[36] In any event, the *choza* or shack where McEwen cares for Florencio Telles and his family was also located at a real place called Rancho Perdido or Lost Ranch.[37]

The novel was hailed for its local-color realism, especially in New Mexico, upon its serialization. The *Santa Fe New Mexican*, for example, commended Rhodes for his depictions of landscape:

> No one can describe this southwestern country as this man. . . . The reader sees in installment number one the Chupadero Mesa, the San Andrés, the Oscuro, the Sandias, Manzanos, Organs, Salinas Peak, the Sacramentos, Sierra Blanca, the Capitans, the Sierra de los Caballos, the Magdalenas, San Mateos, Datils, Guadalupes, the plains of San Agustin, . . . and the glittering White Sands.[38]

Rhodes also limned Las Cruces (a.k.a. Las Uvas) and Belen in the story. The Wilmington, Delaware, *News* opined that *Pasó por Aquí* was "told in so realistic and graphic a manner that one wonders" whether it "originated in Mr. Rhodes' mind" or was "taken from real life."[39] Even the episode in chapter 5 when McEwen "turns his exhausted horse loose" on the range—a ploy by the real bank robbers to distract their pursuers—and saddles a wild

---

Las Cruces Sun-News nearly half a century later ("Local Bank is Robbed in 1900," October 9, 1949, 19).

35 May Rhodes, *The Hired Man on Horseback* (Boston: Houghton Mifflin, 1938), 190.

36 C. L. Sonnichsen, *Tularosa: Last of the Frontier West* (Albuquerque: University of New Mexico Press, 1980), 215.

37 "Annual Gene Rhodes Tour," *Alamogordo News*, May 8, 1963, 3.

38 "Rhodes Again," *Santa Fe New Mexican*, February 19, 1926, 4.

39 "Review of New Books," Wilmington, Del., *News*, May 11, 1927, 4.

steer to escape into the desert seems authentic because Rhodes described the task in painstaking detail.[40]

In *The Desire of the Moth* Rhodes subtly foregrounded the byzantine local politics at the turn of the twentieth century in Las Cruces, the seat of Doña Ana County, home of New Mexico A&M (today New Mexico State University), and today the second largest city in New Mexico. As Rhodes recalled, "Las Cruces was quite mad on politics. It colored every act and thought, distorted them beyond belief."[41] According to historian C. L. Sonnichsen, Rhodes considered Las Cruces "a prime example of what the politicians could do to a good town." Republicans and Democrats "divided the street between them. Each party stayed on its own side and thereby postponed trouble."[42] On his part, according to his biographer W. H. Hutchinson, Rhodes was "a hot-eyed partisan" of the Democrats.[43] In the story, the Republican sheriff—another imaginary character—schemes to defeat the opposition ticket in the next election. That is, he plans to discredit Christopher Foy, the local Democratic leader modeled on Rhodes' friend Oliver Lee (1865–1941), by provoking him to violence and/or framing him for murder.

Looming in the background of the novel is one of the most infamous and unsolved crimes in New Mexico history: the disappearance and presumed murder on the road between Tularosa and Las Cruces in February 1896 of A. J. Fountain, former New Mexico lieutenant governor, leader of Las Cruces Republicans, and member of the secret "Santa Fe Ring" or cabal of Republican politicians who ran the state. Two months later, Garrett was appointed the sheriff of Doña Ana County and in July 1898 he tried to arrest Lee and several others for the Fountain murder. Garrett

---

40 Gary Topping, "The Rise of the Western," *Journal of the West* 19 (January 1980), 32:

"McEwen's robbery of a store and subsequent pursuit by posses are compelling examples of suspenseful writing; even the improbable episode where he turns his exhausted horse loose and saddles a wild steer to hide his trail is convincing."

41 Hutchinson, *A Bar Cross Man*, 135.

42 Sonnichsen, 222, 107.

43 Hutchinson, *A Bar Cross Man*, 44.

and his deputies cornered Lee and the other suspects at Wildy Well, near Orogrande, New Mexico. In a shootout one of Garrett's deputies was mortally wounded and the officers retreated—whereupon Gene Rhodes became tangentially involved in the case. Over the next few months, while Lee and one of his allies negotiated their surrender, Rhodes sheltered them at his ranch in the San Andrés mountains.[44] As George Curry, a former New Mexico territorial governor, noted in his autobiography, Rhodes was "an ardent partisan" and "a constant companion of the hunted men and their 'lookout.'"[45] In March 1899, Lee and his partner finally surrendered to a judge in Las Cruces on the condition they "did not have to surrender to Sheriff Garrett." While they were in custody and during their subsequent trial, the judge appointed Rhodes to help protect them.[46] Lee and his alleged co-conspirators, defended by Albert Fall, were soon acquitted.

Rhodes set his novel, which contains the only reference to the Fountain murder case in any of his writings and then merely in passing, eight years after the "trouble."[47] The fictional sheriff fears that the Democrats led by Kit Foy are poised to sweep into office. As he remarks, "Half the valley is owned by newcomers, men of substance, who, with the votes they influence or control, will decide the election" and "Foy is half a hero with them." True enough: as Sonnichsen reports, "Most of the cattlemen" in Doña Ana County favored the Democrats in 1904 "and so were many interested outsiders."[48] Foy frets correctly, however, that the other side plans to stir the waters "again for political effect" before the fall election. Pringle risks life, limb, and reputation to protect Foy from his political enemies. Even a decade before the publication of *Pasó por Aquí*, the *Los Angeles Times* commended Rhodes for his "magic touch of verisimilitude" in *The Desire of the Moth* "that makes even the daring

44 Hutchinson, *A Bar Cross Man*, 62–63.

45 *George Curry, 1861–1947: An Autobiography* (Albuquerque: University of New Mexico Press, 1958), 109.

46 "Oliver Lee Surrendered," *El Paso Herald*, March 13, 1899, 1.

47 Rhodes, "The Desire of the Moth," *Saturday Evening Post*, February 26, 1916, 4.

48 Sonnichsen, 174.

adventures of men like John Wesley Pringle seem like the natural things to expect."[49]

Rhodes disdained firebrand formula Westerns and refused to write them. His stories rarely feature gunplay or romantic subplots, standard elements of the popular genre. In a word, he shunned love stories. Though he often portrayed women characters, he admitted in 1915 that he could not "put the New Mexico girl on paper. It is the truth I hold most dear that the New Mexico girl is the most lief and dear and lovable of her sex. But I don't understand her." Or as he wrote Webb in 1927, "the reason I do not put love into my stories . . . is that if I did I would be called a sentimental idiot."[50] Or as Charlotte Perkins Gilman asserts, Rhodes was "no feminist" and his women were "just women," though endowed with "character enough."[51] Rhodes modeled Stella Vorhis, Foy's betrothed and the only female character in *Moth*, on Rhoda Williams, a librarian he met in 1920 while living in Los Angeles, or on Turbesé Lummis, the daughter of his friend Charles F. Lummis. He nicknamed Williams "Little Girl" and Lummis "Little Extra," much as in the story Pringle nicknames Stella "Little Next Door."[52] More to the point: Rhodes gleaned the title of the novel from a line "One Word Is Too Often Profaned" by the English romantic poet Percy Bysshe Shelley (1792–1822). In a romantic subtext Rhodes deliberately underdeveloped, "Pringle," an obsolete English contraction for "permanently single," betrays, as Shelley put it, an unfulfilled and hopeless "desire of the moth for the star" or stella.

Both novels were subsequently made into Hollywood movies. *Moth* was twice adapted to silent films, though they both are now lost, the first

---

49 "Romances of Navajo Land," *Los Angeles Times*, October 17, 1920, 58.

50 Hutchinson, *A Bar Cross Man*, 135, 264.

51 Gilman, "A Neglected Author," *Saturday Review of Literature*, August 9, 1924, 38; Hutchinson, *A Bar Cross Man*, 343. Rhodes titled his second novel, "The Little Eohippus," serialized in the *Saturday Evening Post* in November–December 1912, after a line in Gilman's poem "Similar Cases" (1890).

52 Hutchinson, *A Bar Cross Man*, 147, 158; Frank M. Clark, *Sandpapers: The Lives and Letters of Eugene Manlove Rhodes and Charles Fletcher Lummis* (Santa Fe: Sunstone, 1994), 59.

produced in 1917 starring Ruth Clifford and Monroe Salisbury, the second titled *The Wallop* directed by John Ford, starring Harry Carey, released in 1921. In 1948, Joel McCrea starred in an adaptation of *Pasó* filmed on location in New Mexico, including scenes in Gallup and at Inscription Rock and White Sands, titled *Four Faces West*. This treatment suffered from the restrictions imposed on the film industry by the Hays Code, which forbade the "lowering of moral standards" of movie audiences by the depiction of illegal or illicit conduct that is not censured. As a result, *Four Faces West* fudged the depiction of McEwen's bank theft. Lest there be any confusion about the identity of the hero, in the opening scene McEwen rides a white horse. His father faces foreclosure on his ranch and McEwen applies for a loan from the local bank, but he has no collateral—whereupon he forces the banker to approve an unsecured loan at gunpoint. That is, he only "borrows" the money and even signs a note to that effect. In the course of the story he even repays part of the "loan." By the end of the movie, Garrett persuades McEwen to surrender by promising to testify on his behalf at his trial. Not a single gunshot is fired in this atypical Western but, as the Hays Code required, no crime—not even one committed by an otherwise self-sacrificial hero—could go unpunished. Fortunately, the publishers of the period adopted a more relative and relevant standard.

When he died at the age of sixty-five, Rhodes was hailed by his admirers for his illustrious literary career. E. Dana Johnson, the renowned editor of *Santa Fe New Mexican*, wrote the obituary printed in that paper: "His tales are imbued with the true genius of the southwest; and in New Mexico he was much loved largely because of the magic of works in which he could say what so many of us feel about the country."[53] Lansing B. Bloom, editor of the *New Mexico Historical Review*, hailed Rhodes as a "cowboy, student of life, master of prose," and a "seeker after truth and beauty."[54] Western novelist William MacLeod Raine celebrated his friend's stories

53 Johnson, "Good Man and True," *Santa Fe New Mexican*, June 28, 1934, 4.

54 Bloom, "Pasó por Aquí: Eugene Manlove Rhodes 1869–1934," *New Mexico Historical Review* 10 (April 1935), 150.

over a dozen years after his passing: "True in detail and spirit, they mirrored the time and place which created a new way of life with its own code, traditions, vernacular, and social system."[55]

Albuquerque, New Mexico
September 2025

---

55 Raine, "Gene Rhodes as I Knew Him," *Denver Post*, February 8, 1948, magazine, 2.

BIBLIOGRAPHY

Primary Sources

Dearing, Frank V., ed. *Best Novels and Short Stories of Eugene Manlove Rhodes.* Boston and New York: Houghton Mifflin, 1949; rpt. Lincoln: University of Nebraska Press, 1987.

Hutchinson, W. H., ed. *The Rhodes Reader: Stories of Virgins, Villains, and Varmints.* Norman: University of Oklahoma Press, 1957.

Schaefer, Jack, ed. *Out West: A Western Omnibus.* London: Deutsch, 1959.

Secondary Sources

Busby, Mark. "Eugene Manlove Rhodes: Ken Kesey Passed by Here." *Western American Literature* 15 (Summer 1980), 83–92.

Charles, Bula L. (Mrs. Tom). *Tales of the Tularosa.* Alamagordo: Bennett, 1954.

Fife, Jim L. "Two Views of the American West." *Western American Literature* 1 (Spring 1966), 34–42.

Gaston, Edwin W., Jr. *Eugene Manlove Rhodes: Cowboy Chronicler.* Austin: Steck-Vaughn, 1967.

Hutchinson, W. H. *A Bar Cross Man: The Life and Personal Writings of Eugene Manlove Rhodes.* Norman: University of Oklahoma Press, 1956.

Hutchinson, W. H. "Grassfire on the Great Plains: Story of a Literary Battle." *Southwest Review* 41 (Spring 1956), 181–85.

Hutchinson, W. H. "I Pay for What I Break." *Western American Literature* 1 (Summer 1966), 91–96.

Knibbs, Henry H. *The Proud Sheriff.* Norman: University of Oklahoma Press, 1968.

Skillman, Richard, and Jerry C. Hoke. "The Portrait of the New Mexican in the Fiction of Eugene Rhodes." *Western Review* 6 (Spring 1969), 26–36.

A Note on the Texts

Pasó por Aquí was originally serialized in the *Saturday Evening Post*, February 20, 1926, 3–5, 118, 123, 125–26; and February 27, 1926, 22–23, 64, 69. Slightly revised, it was published in a book (pp. 147–259) together with Rhodes' *Once in the Saddle* on April 29, 1927, by Houghton Mifflin of Boston and New York.

The Desire of the Moth was originally serialized in the *Saturday Evening Post*, February 26, 1916, 3–5, 57–58, 61–62; and March 4, 1916, 18–20, 46–47, 50–51. Slightly revised, it was issued as a book on April 15, 1916, by Henry Holt of New York.

PASÓ POR AQUÍ

CHAPTER I

EXCEPTIONS ARE SO INEVITABLE that no rule is without them—except the one just stated. Neglecting fractions, then, not to insult intelligence by specifying the obvious, trained nurses are efficient, skillful, devoted. It is a noble calling. Nevertheless, it is notorious that the official uniform is of reprehensible charm. This regulation is variously explained by men, women and doctors. "No fripperies, curlicues and didos—bully!" say the men. "Ah! Yes! But why? Artful minxes!" say the women, who should know best. "Cheerful influence in the sickroom," say the doctors.

Be that as it may, such uniform Jay wore, spotless and starched, crisp and cool; Jay Hollister, now seated on the wide portico of the Alamogordo Hospital; not chief nurse, but chief ornament, according to many, not only of that hospital but of the great railroad which maintained it. Alamogordo was a railroad town, a new town, a ready-made and highly painted town, direct from Toyland.

Ben Griggs was also a study in white—flannels, oxfords and panama; a privileged visitor who rather overstepped his privileges; almost a fixture in that pleasant colonnade.

"Lamp of life," said Ben, "let's get down to brass tacks. You're homesick!"

"Homesick!" said Jay scornfully. "*Homesick!* I'm heartsick, bankrupt, shipwrecked, lost, forlorn—here in this terrible country, among these dreadful people. Homesick? Why, Ben, I'm just damned!"

"Never mind, heart's delight," said Ben the privileged. "You've got me."

Miss Hollister seemed in no way soothed by this reassuring statement.

"Your precious New Mexico! Sand!" she said. "Sand, snakes, scorpions; wind, dust, glare and heat; lonely, desolate and forlorn!"

"Under the circumstances," said Ben, "you could hardly pay me a greater compliment. 'Whither thou goest, I will go,'[1] and all that. Good girl! This unsolicited tribute—"

"Don't be a poor simpleton," advised the good girl. "I shall stick it out for my year, of course, since I was foolish enough to undertake it. That is all. Don't you make any mistakes. These people shall never be my people."

"No better people on earth. In all the essentials—"

"Oh, who cares anything about essentials?" cried Jay impatiently—voicing, perhaps, more than she knew. "A tin plate will do well enough to eat out of, certainly, if that is what you mean. I prefer china, myself. I'm going back where I can see flowers and green grass, old gardens and sundials."

"I know not what others may say," observed Ben grandly, "but as for me, you take the sundials and give me the sun. Right here, too, where they climb for water and dig for wood. Peevish, my fellow townsman, peevish, waspy, crabbed. You haven't half enough to do. In this beastly climate people simply will not stay sick. They take up their bed and beat it, and you can't help yourself. Nursing is a mere sinecure." His hands were clasped behind his head, his slim length reclined in a steamer chair, feet crossed, eyes half closed, luxurious. "Ah, idleness!" he murmured. "Too bad, too bad! You never were a grouch back home. Rather good company, if anything."

Ben's eyes were blue and dreamy. They opened a trifle wider now, and rolled slowly till they fell upon Miss Hollister, bolt upright and haughty in her chair, her lips pressed in a straight line. She regarded him sternly. He blinked, his hands came from behind his head, he straightened up and adjusted his finger tips to meet with delicate precision. "But the main trouble, the fount and origin of your disappointing conduct is, as hereinbefore said, homesickness. It is, as has been observed, a nobler

1 Ruth 1:16.

pang than indigestion, though the symptoms are of striking similarity. But nostalgia, more than any other feeling, is fatal to the judicial faculties, and I think, my dear towny, that when you look at this fair land, your future home, you regard all things with a jaundiced eye."

"Oh-h!" gasped Jay, hotly indignant. "Look at it yourself! Look at it!"

The hospital was guarded and overhung by an outer colonnade of cottonwoods; she looked through a green archway across the leagues of shimmering desert, somber, wavering and dim; she saw the long bleak range beyond, saw-toothed and gray; saw in the midway levels the unbearable brilliance of the White Sands, a wild dazzle and tumult of light, a blinding mirror with two score miles for diameter.

But Ben's eyes widened with delight, their blue darkened to a deeper blue of exultation, not to be feigned.

"More than beautiful—fascinating," he said.

"Repulsive, hateful, malignant, appalling!" cried Jay Hollister bitterly. "The starved, withered grass, the parched earth, the stunted bushes—miserable, hideous—the abomination of desolation!"

"Girl, by all good rights I ought to shut your wild, wild mouth with kisses four—that's what I orter do—elocutin' that way. But you mean it, I guess." Ben nodded his head sagely. "I get your idea. Blotched and leprous, eh? Thin, starved soil, poisoned and mildewed patches—thorns and dwarfed scrub, red leer of the sun. Oh, *sí*! Like that bird in Browning? Hills like giants at a huntin' lay—the round squat turret—all the lost adventures, my peers—the Dark Tower, weird noises just offstage, increasin' like a bill, I mean a bell—increasin' like a bell,[2] fiddles a-moanin', 'O-o-o-h-h-h! What did you do-o-o with your summer's wa-a-a-ges? So this is Paris!'[3] Yes, yes! But why not shed the second-hand stuff and come down to workaday?"

"Ben Griggs," said Miss Hollister with quiet and deadly conviction, "you are absolutely the most blasphemous wretch that ever walked in shoe leather. You haven't anything even remotely corresponding to a soul."

---

2 Griggs alludes to Robert Browning's "Childe Roland to the Dark Tower Came" (1855).

3 An apparent anomaly in the text: the movie *So This is Paris* was released by Warner Brothers in 1926.

"When we are married," said Ben, and paused, reflecting. "That is, if I don't change my mind—"

"Married!" said Miss Hollister derisively. "*When! You!*" Her eyes scorned him.

"Woman," said Ben, "beware! You make utter confusion with the parts of speech. You make mere interjections of pronouns, prepositions and verbs and everything. You use too many shockers. More than that—mark me, my lass—isn't it curious that no one has ever thought to furnish printed words with every phonograph record of a song? Just a little sheet of paper—why, it needn't cost more than a penny apiece at the outside. Then we could know what it was all about."

"The way you hop from conversational crag to crag," said Jay, "is beyond all praise."

"Oh, well, if you insist, we can go back to our marriage again."

"My poor misguided young friend," said Jay, "make no mistakes. I put up with you because we played together when we were kids, and because we are strangers here in a strange land, townies together—"

Ben interrupted her. "Two tawny townies twisting twill together!" he chanted happily, beating slow time with a gentle finger. "Twin turtles twitter tender twilight twaddle. Twice twenty travelers—"

"Preposterous imbecile!" said Jay, dimpling nevertheless adorably. "Here is something to put in your little book. Jay Hollister will never marry an idler and a wastrel. Why, you're not even a ne'er-do-well. You're a do-nothing, net."

"All the world loves a loafer," Ben protested. "Still, as Alice remarked, if circumstances were different they would be quite otherwise.[4] If frugal industry—"

"There comes your gambler friend," said Jay coldly.

---

4 Griggs apparently refers to the "moral" offered by the Duchess in chapter 9 of Lewis Carroll's *Alice in Wonderland* (1865): "Never imagine yourself not to be otherwise than what it might appear to others that what you were or might have been was not otherwise than what you had been would have appeared to them to be otherwise." Alice replies: "I think I should understand that better if I had it written down."

"Who, Monte? Where?" Ben turned eagerly.

"Across the street. No, the other way." Though she fervently disapproved of Monte, Jay was not sorry for the diversion. It was daily more difficult to keep Ben in his proper place, and she had no desire to discuss frugal industry.

"Picturesque rascal, what? Looking real pleased about something too. Say, girl, you have made me forget something I was going to tell you."

"He is laughing to himself," said Jay.

"I believe he is, at that." Ben raised his voice. "Hi, Monte! Come over and tell us the joke."

CHAPTER II

MONTE'S MOTHER HAD KNOWN him as Rosalio Marquez. The overname was professional. He dealt monte[5] wisely but not too well. He was nearing thirty-five, the easiest age of all; he was slender and graceful; he wore blue serge and a soft black hat, low crowned and wide brimmed. He carried this hat in his hand as he came up the steps. He bowed courteously to Jay, with murmured greetings in Spanish, soft syllables of lingering caress; he waved a friendly salute to Ben.

"Yes, indeed," said Ben. "With all my heart. Your statement as to the beauty of the day is correct in every particular, and it affords me great pleasure to indorse an opinion so just. But, after all, dear heart, that is hardly the point, is it? The giddy jest, the merry chuckles—those are the points on which we greatly desire information.

Monte hesitated, almost imperceptibly, a shrewd questioning in his eyes.

"Yes, have a chair," said Jay, "and tell us the joke."

"Thees is good, here, thank you," said Monte. He sat on the top step and hung the black hat on his knee; his face lit up with soft low laughter. "The joke? Oh, eet ees upon the sheriff, Jeem Hunter.[6] I weel tell eet."

He paused to consider. In his own tongue Monte's speech sounded

5 A type of three-card poker game.

6 Jim Hunter (1858–1938), Rhodes' friend and the first elected sheriff of Otero County in New Mexico, ran as a Democrat in 1900, served until 1905, and was re-elected as a Socialist in 1911.

uncommonly like a pack of firecrackers lit at both ends. In English it was leisured, low and thoughtful. The unslurred vowels, stressed and piquant, the crisp consonants, the tongue-tip accents—these things combined to make the slow caressing words into something rich and colorful and strange, all unlike our own smudged and neutral speech. The customary medium of the Southwest between the two races is a weird and lawless hodge-podge of the two tongues—a barbarous lingua franca.

As Miss Hollister had no Spanish, Monte drew only from his slender stock of English; and all unconsciously he acted the story as he told it.

"When Jeem was a leetle, small boy," said Monte, his hand knee-high to show the size in question, "he dream manee times that he find thoss marbles—oh, many marbles! That mek heem ver' glad, thees nize dream. Then he get older"—Monte's hand rose with the sheriff's maturity—"and sometime he dream of find money lak thoss marble. And now Jeem ees grown and sheriff—an' las' night he come home, ver' late, ver' esleepy. I weel tell you now how eet ees, but Jeem he did not know eet. You see, Melquiades, he have a leetle, litla game." He glanced obliquely at Miss Hollister, his shoulders and down-drawn lips expressed apology for the little game, and tolerance for it. "Just neeckels and dimes. An' some fellow he go home weener, and there ees hole een hees pocket. But Jeem he do not know. Bueno, Jeem has been to Tularosa, Mescalero, Fresnal, all places, to leef word to look out for thees fellow las' week what rob the bank at Belen, and he arrive back on a freight train las' night, mebbe so about three in the morning—oh, veree tired, ver' esleepy. So when he go up the street een the moonlight he see there a long streeng of neeckels and dimes under hees feet." Without moving, Monte showed the homeward progress of that drowsy man and his faint surprise. "So Jeem, he laugh and say, 'There ees that dream again.' And he go on. But bimeby he steel see thoss neeckels, and he peench heemself, so—and he feel eet." Monte's eyes grew round with astonishment. "And he bend heemself to peek eet, and eet ees true money, and not dreaming at all! Yais. He go not back, but on ahead he peek up one dollar seexty-five cents of thees neeckels and dimes."

"I hadn't heard of any robbery, Monte," said Ben. "What about it?"

"Yes, and where is Belen?" said Jay. "Not around here, surely. I've never heard of the place."

"Oh, no—*muy lejos*—a long ways. Belen, what you call Bethlehem, ees yonder this side of Albuquerque, a leetle. I have been there manee times, but not estraight—round about." He made a looping motion of his hand to illustrate. "Las Vegas, and then down, or by Las Cruces, and then up. Eet is hundred feefty, two hundred miles in estraight line—I do not know."

"Anybody hurt?" asked Ben.

"Oh, no—no fuss! Eet ees veree funnee. Don Numa Frenger[7] and Don Nestor Trujillo,[8] they have there beeg estore to sell all theengs, leetle bank, farms, esheep ranch, freighting for thoss mines, buy wool and hides—all theengs for get the monee what ees there een thees place. And las' week, maybe Friday, Saturday, Nestor he ees go to deenair, and Numa Frenger ees in the estore, *solito*.

"Comes een a customer, *un Colorado*—es-scusa me, a redhead. He buy tomatoes, cheese, crackers, sardines, sooch things, and a nose bag, and he ask to see shotgun. Don Numa, he exheebit two, three, and thees red he peek out nize shotgun. So he ask for shells, bird-eshot, buck-eshot, and he open the buck-eshot and sleep two shells een barrel, and break eet to throw out thoss shell weeth extractor, and sleep them een again. 'Eet work fine!' he say. 'Have you canteen?'

"Then Numa Frenger he tek long pole weeth hook to get thoss canteen where eet hang from the viga, the r-rafter, the beams. And when he get eet, he turn around an' thees estranger ees present thees shotgun at hees meedle. Yais.

"'Have you money een your esafe?' say the *estranjero*, the estr-ranger. And Numa ees bite hees mouth. 'Of your kindness,' say the customer, 'weel you get heem? I weel go weeth you?'

---

7 After the publication of *Pasó por Aquí*, Rhodes joked that Numa Charles Frenger (1876–1945), an Alamogordo Democrat, former Rough Rider, and judge of the Third Judicial District in New Mexico, who is described in the story as "a ver' fat man," had sworn "he will shoot me on sight" (Hutchinson, *A Bar Cross Man*, 243).

8 Nestor Trujillo resided in Rio Arriba County, New Mexico, in 1904.

"So they get thees money from the esafe. And thees one weel not tek onlee the paper money. 'Thees gold an' seelver ees so heav-ee,' he tell Numa Frenger. 'I weel not bozzer.' Then he pay for those theengs of which he mek purchase an' correc' Don Numa when he mek meestake in the *adición*, and get hees change back. And then he say to Numa, 'Weel you not be so good to come to eshow me wheech ees best road out from thees town to the ford of the reever?' And Numa, he ees ge-nash hees teeth, but there ees no *remedio*.

"And so they go walking along thees lane between the orchards, these two togezzer, and the leetle bir-rds esing een the *árboles*[9]—thees red fellow laughing and talkin' weeth Numa, ver' gay—leading hees horse by the bridle, and weeth the shotgun een the crook of hees arm. So the people loog out from the doors of their house and say, 'Ah! Don Numa ees diverrt heemself weeth hees friend.

"And when they have come beyond the town, thees fellow ees mount hees horse. 'For your courtesy,' he say, 'I thank you. At your feet,' he say. 'Weeth God!' And he ride off laughing, and een a leetle way he toss hees shotgun een a bush, and he ride on to cross the reever eslow. But when Numa Frenger sees thees, he run queeckly, although he ees a ver' fat man, an' not young; he grab thees gun, he point heem, he pull the triggle—Nozzing! He break open the gun to look wizzen side—Nozzing! *O caballteros y conciudadanos*!" Monte threw down the gun; both hands grabbed his black locks and tugged with the ferocity of despair.

"Ah-h! What a lovely cuss word," cried Jay. "How trippingly it goes upon the tongue. I must learn that. Say it again!"

"But eet ees not a bad word, that," said Monte sheepishly. "Eet ees onlee idle word, to feel up. When thees *politicos* go up an' down, talking nonsense een the nose, when they weesh to theenk of more, then they say with emotion, '*O caballeros y conciudadanos*'; that ees, 'gentlemen and fellow ceetizens.' No more."

"Well, now, the story?" said Ben. "He crossed the river, going east—was that it?"

---

9 trees

"Oh, yes. Well, when Numa Frenger see that thees gun ees emptee, he ees ver' angree man. He ees more enr-rage heemself for that than for all what gone befor-re. He ees arrouse all Belen, he ees send telegraph to Sabinal, La Joya, Socorro, San Marcial, ever wheech way, to mek queek the posse, to send queek to the mesa to catch thees man, to mek *proclamatión* to pay for heem three thousand dollar of rewar-rd. 'Do not keel heem, I entr-reat you,' say Don Numa. 'Breeng heem back. I want to fry heem.'"

"Now isn't that New Mexico for you?" demanded Jay "A man commits a barefaced robbery, and you make a joke of it."

Monte pressed the middle finger of his right hand firmly into the palm of his left, pressed as if to hold something there, and looked up under his brows at Miss Hollister.

"Then why do you laugh?" said Monte.

"You win," said Jay. "Go on with the story."

"Well, then," said Monte, "thees fellow he go up on the high plain on thees side of the reever, and he ride east and south by Sierra Montoso, and over the mountains of Los Piños, and he mek to go over Chupadero Mesa to thoss ruins of Gran Quivira. But he ride onlee *poco á poco*,[10] easalee. And already a posse from La Joya, San Acacia is ride up the Alamillo Cañon, and across the plain." His swift hands fashioned horseman, mountain, mesa and plain. "Page Otero[11] and six, five other men. And they ride veree fast so that already they pass in front of him to the south, and are now before heem on Chupadero, and there they see heem. Eet ees almost sundown.

"*Immediatamente* he turn and go back. And their horses are not so tired lak hees horse, and they spread out and ride fast, and soon they are about to come weethen gunshot weeth the rifle. And when he see eet, thees *colorado* ees ride oopon a reedge that all may see, and he tek that paper money from the nose bag at the head of the saddle and he toss eet up—pouf! The weend is blow gentle and thees money it go joomp, joomp, here, there, een

10 little by little

11 Page B. Otero (1858–1933), son and brother of former New Mexico governors, was a mounted policeman, deputy sheriff, and state game warden.

the booshes. Again he ride a leetle way, and again he scatter thees money lak a man to feed the hen een hees yard. So then he go on away, thees red one. And when thees posse come to that place, thees nize money is go hop, hop, along the ground and over the booshes. There ees feefty-dollar beel een the mesquite, there ees twenty-dollar beel een the tar-bush, there ees beels blow by, roll by, slide by. So thees posse ees deesmount heemself to peek heem, *muy enérgico*—lively. And the weend ess come up faster at sundown, *como siempre.*[12] 'Come on!' says Page Otero. 'Come on, thees fellow weel to escape!' Then the posse loog up surprise, and say, 'Who, me?' and they go on to peek up thees monee. So that redhead get clear away thees time."

"Did they get all the money?" asked Ben.

"Numa he say yes. He do not know just how mooch thees bandit ees take, but he theenk they breeng back all, or most nearly all."

"Do they know who he was?" asked Jay.

"*Por cierto,*[13] no. But from the deescreepcion and hees horse and saddle, they theenk eet ees a cowboy from Quemado, name—I cannot to pr-ronounce thees name, Meester Ben. You say heem. I have eet here een 'La Voz del Pueblo.'"[14] From a hip pocket he produced a folded newspaper printed in Spanish, and showed Ben the place.

"Ross McEwen—about twenty-five or older, red hair, gray eyes, five feet nine inches—humph!" he returned the paper. "Will they catch him, do you think?"

Monte considered. He looked slowly at the far dim hills; he bent over to watch an inch-high horseman at his feet, toiling through painful immensities.

"The world ees ver' beeg een thees country," he said at last. "I theenk most mebbe not. *Quién sabe?*[15] Onlee thees fellow must have water—and there ees not much water. Numa Frenger ees send now to all places, to Leencoln County, to Jeem Hunter here, and he meks everyone to loog

12 as usual

13 by the way

14 *The Voice of the People*, a Spanish-language newspaper published in Santa Fe.

15 Who knows?

out, to Pat Garrett in Doña Ana Countee, and Pat watches by Parker Lake and the pass of San Agustin; to El Paso, and they watch there most of all that he pass not to Mexico Viejo. Eet may be at some water place they get heem. Or that he get them. He seem lak a man of some enter-pr-rize, no?" He rose to go. "But I have talk too much. I mus' go now to my beesness."

"A poor business for a man as bright as you are," said Jay, and sniffed.

"But I geeve a square deal," said Monte serenely. "At your feet, señorita! Unteel then, Meester Ben."

"Isn't he a duck? I declare, it's a shame to laugh at his English," said Jay.

"Don't worry. He gets to hear our Spanish, even if he is too polite to laugh."

"I hate to think of that man being chased for blood money," said Jay. "Hunter and that Pat Garrett you think so much of are keen after that reward, it seems. It is dreadful the way these people here make heroes out of their killers and man hunters."

"Let's get this straight," said Ben. "You're down on the criminal for robbing and down on the sheriff for catching him. Does that sound like sense? If there was no reward offered, it's the sheriff's duty to catch him, isn't it? And if there is a reward, it's still his duty. The reward doesn't make him a man hunter. Woman, you ain't right in your head. And as for Pat Garrett and some of these other old-timers—they're enjoying temporary immortality right now. They've become a tradition while they still live. Do you notice how all these honest-to-goodness old-timers talk? All the world is divided into three parts. One part is old-timers and the other two are not. The most clannish people on earth. And that brings us, by graceful and easy stages, to the main consideration, which I want to have settled before I go. And when I say settled I mean that nothing is ever settled till it is settled right—get me?" He stood up; as Jay rose he took her hands. "If circumstances were otherwise, Jay?"

She avoided his eyes. "Don't ask me now. I don't know, Ben—honest, I don't. You mustn't pester me now. It isn't fair when I'm so miserable." She pulled her hands away.

"Gawd help all poor sailors on a night like this!" said Ben fervently.

"Listen, sister, I'm going to work, see? Goin' to fill your plans and specifications, every one, or bust a tug."

"I see you at it," jeered Jay, with an unpleasant laugh. "Work? You?"

"Me. I, myself. A faint heart never filled a spade flush," said Ben. "Going to get me a job and keep it. Lick any man that tries to fire me. Put that in your hope chest. Bye-bye. At your feet!"

As he went down the street his voice floated back to her:

But now my hair is falling out,
And down the hill we'll go,
And sleep together at the foot—
John Barleycorn, my Jo![16]

16 Rhodes' parody of the ballad "John Anderson, my jo, John" (1782) by the Scottish poet Robert Burns (1759–1796).

CHAPTER III

A HIGH BROAD TABLELAND lies east of the Rio Grande, and mountains make a long unbroken wall to it, with cliffs that front the west. This mesa is known locally as El Corredor. It is a pleasing and wholesome country. Zacatón[17] and salt grass are gray green upon the level plain, checkered with patches of bare ground, white and glaring. On those bare patches, when the last rains fell, weeks, months or years ago, an oozy paste filmed over the glossy levels, glazed by later suns, cracking at last to shards like pottery. But in broken country, on ridges and slopes, was a thin turf of buffalo and mesquite grass, curly, yellow and low. There was iron beneath this place and the sand of it was red, the soil was ruddy white, the ridges and the lower hill slopes were granite red, yellowed over with grass. Even the high crowning cliffs were faintly cream, not gray, as limestone is elsewhere. Sunlight was soft and mellow there, sunset was red upon these cliffs. And Ross McEwen fled down that golden corridor.

If he had ridden straight south he might have been far ahead by this time, well on the road to Mexico. But his plan had been to reach the Panhandle of Texas; he had tried for easting and failed. Three times he had sought to work through the mountain barrier to the salt plains—a bitter country of lava flow and sinks, of alkali springs, salt springs, magnesia springs, soda springs; of soda lakes, salt lakes, salt marshes, salt creeks; of rotten and crumbling ground, of greasy sand, of chalk that powdered and

17 A wiry grass native to desert climates.

rose on the lightest airs, to leave no trace that a fugitive had passed this way.

He had been driven back once by posse on Chupadero. Again at night he had been forced back by men who did not see him. He had tried to steal through by the old Ozanne stage road over the Oscuro, and found the pass guarded; and the last time, today, had been turned back by men that he did not even see. In the mouth of Mockingbird Pass he had found fresh-shod tracks of many horses going east. Mockingbird was held against him.

He could see distinctly, and in one eye-flight, every feature of a country larger than all England. He could look north to beyond Albuquerque, past the long ranges of Manzano, Montoso, Sandia, Oscuro; southward, between his horse's ears, the northern end of the San Andrés was high and startling before him, blue black with cedar brake and piñon, except for the granite-gold top of Salinas Peak, the great valley of the Jornado del Muerto, the Journey of the Dead, which lay between the San Andrés and the Rio Grande.

And beyond the river was a bright enormous expanse, bounded only by the crest of the dozen ranges that made the crest of the Continental Divide—Dátil, Magdalena, San Mateo, the Black Range, the Mimbres, Florida.

Between, bordering the midway river, other mountain ranges lay tangled: Cuchillo Negro, Cristobál, Sierra de los Caballos, Doña Ana, Robelero. It was over the summits of these ranges that he saw the Continental Divide.

Here was irony indeed. With that stupendous panorama outspread before him, he was being headed off, driven, herded! He cocked an eyebrow aslant at the thought, and spoke of it to his horse, who pricked back an ear in attention. He was a honey-colored horse, and his name was Miél; which is, by interpretation, Honey.

"Wouldn't you almost think, sweetness," said Ross McEwen in a plaintive drawl, "that there was enough elbowroom here to satisfy every reasonable man? And yet these lads are crowdin' me like a cop after an alley cat."

He sensed that an unusual effort was being made to take him, and he smiled—a little ruefully—at the reflection that the people at Mockingbird might well have been mere chance comers upon their lawful occasions, and with no designs upon him, no knowledge of him. Every man was a possible enemy. He was out of law.

This was the third day of his flight. The man was still brisk and bold, the honey-colored horse was still sturdy, but both lacked something of the sprightly resilience they had brought to the fords of Belen. There had been brief grazing and scant sleep, night riding, doubling and twisting to slip into lonely water holes. McEwen had chosen, as the lesser risk, to ride openly to Prairie Springs. He had found no one there and had borrowed grub for himself and several feeds of corn for the Honey horse. There had been no fast riding, except for the one brief spurt with the posse at Chupadero. But it had been a steady grind, doubly tiresome that they might not keep to the beaten trails. Cross-country traveling on soft ground is rough on horseflesh.

And now they left the plain and turned through tar-bush up the long slope to the San Andrés. A thousand ridges and hollows came plunging and headlong against them. And suddenly the tough little horse was tiring, failing.

Halfway to the hill foot they paused for a brief rest. High on their slim lances, banners of yucca blossoms were white and waxen, and wild bees hummed to their homes in the flower stalks of last year; flaunting afar, cactus flowers flamed crimson or scarlet through the black tar-bush.

Long since McEwen had given up the Panhandle. He planned now to bear far to the southeast, crossing the salt plains below the White Sands to the Guadalupe Mountains, where they straddled the boundary between the territory and Texas, and so east to the Staked Plains. He knew the country ahead, or had known it ten years before. But there would be changes. There was a new railroad, so he had heard, from El Paso to Tularosa, and so working north toward the states. There would be other things, too—new ranches, and all that. For sample, behind him, just where this long slope merged with the flats, three unexpected windmills, each five miles from the other, had made a line across his path; he had made a weary detour to pass unseen.

The San Andrés made here a twenty-mile offset where they joined the

Oscuro, with the huge round mass of Salinas Peak as their mutual corner. Lava Gap, the meeting-place of the two ranges, was now directly at his left and ten miles away. The bleak and mile-high walls of it made a frame for the tremendous picture of Sierra Blanca, sixty long miles to the east, with a gulf of nothingness between. Below that nothingness, as McEwen knew, lay the black lava river of the Mai Pais. But Lava Gap was not for him. Unless pursuit was quite abandoned, Lava Gap and Dripping Springs would be watched and guarded. He was fenced in by probabilities.

But the fugitive was confident yet, and by no means at the end of his resources. He knew a dim old Indian trail over a high pass beyond Salinas Peak. It started at Grapevine Spring, Captain Jack Crawford's ranch.[18] "And at Grapevine," said Ross aloud, "I'll have to buy, beg, borrow, or get me a horse. Hope there's nobody at home. If there's anyone there I'll have to get his gun first and trade afterwards. Borrowing horses is not highly recommended, but it beats killing 'em."

To the right and before him the Jornado was hazy, vast, and mysterious. To the right and behind him, the lava flow of Pascual sprawled black and sinister in the lowlands; and behind him—Far behind him, far below him, a low line of dust was just leaving the central windmill of those three new ranches, a dozen miles away. McEwen watched this dust with some interest while he rolled and lit a cigarette. He drank the last water from his canteen.

"Come on, me bold outlaw," he said, "keep moving. You've done made your bed, but these hellhounds won't let you sleep in it." He put foot to stirrup; he stroked the Honey horse.

"Miél, old man, you tough it out four or five miles more, and your troubles will be over. Me for a fresh horse at Grapevine, come hell or high water. Take it easy. No hurry. Just shuffle along."

The pursuing dust did not come fast, but it came straight his way. "I'll bet a cooky," said Ross sagely, "that some of these gay bucks have got a spyglass. I wonder if that ain't against the rules? And new men throwin' in

18 Jack W. Crawford (1847–1917), "the poet scout," ranched in Sierra County, New Mexico.

with them at every ranch. I reckon I would, too, if it wasn't for this red topknot of mine. Why couldn't they meet up with some other redheaded hellion and take him back? Wouldn't that be just spiffin'? One good thing, anyway—I didn't go back to the Quemado country. Some of the boys would sure have got in Dutch, hidin' me out. This is better."

He crossed the old military road that had once gone through Lava Gap to Fort Stanton; he smiled at the shod tracks there; he came to the first hills, pleasingly decorated with bunches of mares—American mares, gentle mares—Corporal Tanner's mares.[19] He picked a bunch with four or five saddle horses in it and drove them slowly up Grapevine Cañon. The Miél horse held up his head and freshened visibly. He knew what this meant. The sun dropped behind the hills. It was cool and fresh in Grapevine.

The outlaw took his time. He had an hour or more. He turned for a last look at the north and the cliffs of Oscuro Mountain blazing in the low sun to fiery streamers of red light. You would have seen, perhaps, only a howling wilderness, but this man was to look back, waking and in dream, and to remember that brooding and sunlit silence as the glowing heart of the world. From this place alone he was to be an exile.

"Nice a piece of country as ever laid outdoors," said Ross McEwen. "I've seen some several places where it would be right pleasant to have a job along with a bunch of decent punchers—good grub and all that, mouth organ by the firelight after supper—Or herding sheep."

Grapevine Spring is at the very head of the cañon. To east, south and west the hills rise directly from the corral fences. McEwen drove the mares into the water pen and called loudly to the house. The hail went unanswered. Eagles screamed back from a cliff above him.

"A fool for luck," said McEwen.

He closed the bars, he gave Miél his first installment of water. Then he went to the house. It was unlocked and there was no one there. The ashes on the hearth were cold. He borrowed two cans of beans and some bacon. There was a slender store of corn, and he borrowed one feed of this to

---

19 James R. Tanner (1844–1927), a Civil War veteran, lobbied for military veterans' rights and served briefly as army pension commissioner in 1889.

make tomorrow's breakfast for the new horse he was soon to acquire. He found an old saddle and he borrowed that, with an old bridle as well; he brought his own to replace them; he lit the little lamp on the table and grinned happily.

"They'll find Miél and my saddle and the light," he said, "and they'll make sure I've taken to the brush." He went back to the pen, he roped and saddled a saddle-marked brown, broad chested and short coupled, unshod. Shod tracks are too easily followed. Then he scratched his red head and grinned again. The pen was built of poles laid in panels, except at the front; the cedar brake grew to the very sides of it. He went to the back and took down two panels, laying the poles aside; he let the mares drift out there, seeing to it that some of them went around by the house, and the rest on the other side of the pen. It was almost dark by now.

"There," he said triumphantly. "The boys will drive in a bunch of stock when they come, for remounts, and they'll go right on through. Fine mess in the dark. And it'll puzzle them to find which way I went with all these tracks. Time I was gone."

He came back to the watering-trough; he washed his hands and face and filled his canteen; he went on where Miél stood weary and huddled in the dusk. His hand was gentle on that drooping neck.

"Miél, old fellow," he said, "you've been one good little horse. *Bueno suerte.*"[20] He led the brown to the bars. "I hate a fool," said Ross McEwen.

He took down the bars and rode into the cedar brush at right angles to the cañon, climbing steadily from the first. It was a high and desperate pass, and branches had grown across the unused trail; long before he had won halfway to the summit he heard, far below him, the crashing of horses in the brush, the sound of curses and laughter. The pursuit had arrived at Grapevine.

He topped the summit of that nameless pass an hour later, and turned down the dark cañon to the east—to meet grief at once. Since his time a cloud-burst had been this way. Where there had once been fair footing the flood had cut deep and wide, and every semblance of soil had washed

---

20 Good luck.

away, leaving only a wild moraine, a loose rubble of rocks and tumbled boulders. But it was the only way. The hillsides were impossibly steep and sidelong, glassy granite and gneiss, or treacherous slides of porphyry. Ross led his horse. Every step was a hazard in that narrow and darkened place, with crumbling ridge and pit and jump off, with windrows of smooth round rock to roll and turn under their feet. It took the better part of two hours to win through the narrows, perhaps two miles. The cañon widened then, the hillsides were lower and Ross could ride again, picking his doubtful way in the starlight. He turned on a stepladder of hills to the north, and came about midnight to Dripstone, high in a secret hollow of the hills. The prodigious bulk of Salinas loomed mysterious and incredible above him in the starlight.

He tied the brown horse securely and named him Porch Climber.[21] He built a tiny fire and toasted strips of bacon on the coals. Then he spread out his saddle blankets with hat and saddle for pillow, and so lay down to untroubled sleep.

21 Slang for a burglar or second-story man. That is, McEwen identifies his horse as a type of thief.

CHAPTER IV

HE AWOKE IN THAT quiet place before the first stirring of dawn. A low thin moon was in the sky and the mountains were dim across the east. He washed his eyes out with water from the canteen. He made a nose bag from the corn sack and hung it on Porch Climber's brown head. The Belen nose bag had gone into the discard days before. He washed out the empty bean can for coffee-pot. He built a fire of twigs and hovered over it while his precious coffee came to a boil; his coat was thin and the night air was fresh, almost chilly. He smacked his lips over the coffee, he saddled and watered Porch Climber at Dripstone and refilled his canteen there. The Porch Climber drank sparingly.

"Better fill up, old-timer," Ross advised him. "You're sure going to need it."

Knuckled ridges led away from Salinas like fingers of a hand. The eastern flat was some large fraction of a mile nearer to sea level than the high plain west of the mountain, and these ridges were massive and steep accordingly. He made his way down one of them. The plain was dark and cold below him; the mountains took shape and grew, the front range of the Rockies—Capitan, Carrizozo, Sierra Blanca, Sacramento, with Guadalupe low and dim in the south; the White Sands were dull and lifeless in the midway plain. Bird twitter was in the air. Rabbits scurried through the brush, a quail whirred by and sent back a startled call; crimson streaks shot up the sky, and day grew broad across the silent levels. The cut banks of Salt Creek appeared, wandering away southwest toward the marshes. Low and far against the black base of the Sacramento, white feathers lifted and fluffed, the smoke of the first fires at Tularosa, fifty miles away. Flame tipped the far-off crests, the sun leaped up from behind the mountain wall, the level light struck on the White Sands, glanced from those burnished bevels and splashed on the western cliffs; the desert day blazed over this new half-world.

He had passed a few cows on the ridges, but now, as he came close to the flats, he was suddenly aware of many cattle before him, midges upon the vast plain; more cattle than he had found on the western side of the mountains. He drew rein, instantly on the alert, and began to quarter the scene with a keen scrutiny. At once a silver twinkling showed to northward—the steel fans of a windmill, perhaps six miles out from the foot of the main mountain. His eye moved slowly across the plain. He was shocked to find a second windmill tower some six or eight miles south of the first, keeping at the same distance from the hills, and when he made out the faint glimmer of a third, far in the south, he gave way to indignation. It was a bald plain with no cover for the quietly disposed, except a few clumps of soapweed here and there. And this line of windmills was precisely the line of the road to El Paso. Where he had expected smooth going he would have to keep to the roughs; to venture into the open was to court discovery. He turned south across the ridges.

He had talked freely to Miél, but until now he had been reticent with Porch Climber, who had not yet won his confidence. At this unexpected reverse he opened his heart.

"Another good land gone wrong," he said. "I might have known it. This side of Salt Creek is only half-bad cow country, so of course it's all settled up, right where we want to go. No one lives east of Salt Creek, not even sheep herders. And we couldn't possibly make it, goin' on the other side of Salt Creek with all that marsh country and the hell of the White Sands. Why, this is plumb ridiculous!"

He meditated for a while upon his wrongs and then broke out afresh: "When I was here, the only water east of the mountains was the Wildy Well at the corner of the damn White Sands. Folks drove along the road, and when they wanted water they went up in the hills. It's no use to cross over to Tularosa. They'll be waiting for us there. No, sir, we've pointedly got to skulk down through the brush. And you'll find it heavy going, up one ridge and down another, like a flea on a washboard."

Topping the next ridge, he reined back swiftly into a hollow place. He dismounted and peered through a mesquite bush, putting the branches aside to look. A mile to the south two horsemen paced soberly down a ridge—and it was a ridge which came directly from the pass to Grapevine.

"Now ain't them the bright lads?" said the runaway, divided between chagrin and admiration. "What are you going to do with fellows like that? I ask you. I left plain word that I done took to the hills afoot, without the shadow of a doubt. Therefore they reasoned I hadn't. They've coppered every bet. Now that's what I call clear thinkin'. I reckon some of 'em did stay there, but these two crossed over that hell-gate at night, just in case.

"I'll tell a man they had a ride where that cloud-burst was. Say, they'll tell their grandchildren about that—if they live that long, which I misdoubt, the way they're carryin' on. This gives me what is technically known as the willies. Hawse," said McEwen, "let's us tarry a spell and see what these hirelin' bandogs are goin' to do now."

He took off the bridle and saddle, he staked Porch Climber to rest and graze while he watched. What the bandogs did was to ride straight to the central windmill, where smoke showed from the house. McEwen awaited developments. Purely from a sense of duty he ate the other can of beans while he waited.

"They'll take word to every ranch," he prophesied gloomily. "Leave a man to watch where there isn't anyone there—take more men along when they find more than one at a well. Wish I was a drummer."

His prognostications were verified. After a long wait, which meant breakfast, a midget horseman rode slowly north towards the first windmill. A little later two men rode slowly south towards the third ranch.

"That's right, spread the news, dammit, and make everybody hate you," said Ross. He saddled and followed them, paralleling their course, but keeping to the cover of the brush.

It was heavy and toilsome going, boulders and rocks alternating with soft ground where Porch Climber's feet went through; gravel, coarse sand or piled rocks in the washes; tedious twisting in the brush and wearisome windings where a bay of open country forced a detour. He passed by the mouths of Good Fortune, Antelope and Cottonwood cañons, struggling through their dry deltas; he drew abreast of the northern corner of the White Sands. The reflection of it was blinding, yet he found it hard to hold his eyes away. The sun rode high and hot. McEwen consulted his canteen.

More than once or twice came the unwelcome thought that he might take to the hill country, discard Porch Climber and hide by some inaccessible seep or pothole until pursuit died down. But he was a stubborn man, and his heart was set upon Guadalupe; he had an inborn distaste for a diet of chance rabbit and tuna fruit—or, perhaps, slow deer without salt. A stronger factor in his decision—although he hardly realized it—was the horseman's hatred for being set afoot. He could hole in safely; there was little doubt of that. But when he came out of the hole, how then? A man from nowhere, on foot, with no past and no name and a long red beard—that would excite remark. He fingered the stubble on his cheeks with that reflection. Yes, such a man would be put to it to account for himself—and he would have to show up sometime, somewhere. The green Cottonwood of Independent Spring showed high on the hill to his right. He held on to the south.

And now he came to the mouth of Sulphur Springs Cañon. Beyond here a great bay of open plain flowed into the hill foot under Kaylor Mountain; and midmost of that bay was another windmill, a long low house, spacious corrals. McEwen was sick of windmills. But this one was close under the mountain, far west of the line of the other ranches and of the El Paso road; McEwen saw with lively interest that his pursuers left the road and angled across the open to this ranch. That meant dinner.

"Honesty," said McEwen with conviction, "is the best policy. Dinnertime for some people, but only noon for me. . . . And how can these enterprisin' chaps be pursuin' me when they're in front? That isn't reasonable. Who ever heard of deputies goin' ahead and the bandit taggin' along behind? That's not right. It's not moral. I'm goin' around. Besides, if I don't this thing is liable to go on always, just windmills and windmills—to Mexico City—Peru—Chile. I'm plumb tired of windmills. Porch Climber," said McEwen, "have you got any gift of speed? Because, just as soon as these two sheriff men get to that ranch and have time to go in the house, you and me are going to drift out quiet and unostentatious across the open country till we hit the banks of the Salt Marsh. And if these fellows look out and see us you've just got to run for it. And they can maybe get fresh horses too. But if they don't see us we'll be right. We'll drift south under cover of the bank and get ahead of 'em while they stuff their paunches."

Half an hour later he turned Porch Climber's head to the east, and rode sedately across the smooth plain, desiring to raise no dust. Some three miles away, near where he crossed the El Paso road, grew a vigorous motte of mesquite trees. Once beyond that motte, he kept it lined up between him and the ranch; and so came unseen to where the plain broke away to the great marsh which rimmed the basin of the White Sands.

In the east the White Sands billowed in great dry dunes above the level of the plain, but the western half was far below that level, and waterbound. This was the home of mirages; they spread now all their pomp of palm and crystal lake and fairy hill. McEwen turned south along the margin. Here, just under the bank, the ground was moist, almost wet, and yet firm footing, like a road of hard rubber. He brought Porch Climber to a long-reaching trot, steady and smooth; he leaned forward in his stirrups and an old song came to his lips, unsummoned. He sang it with loving mockery, in a nasal but not unpleasing barytone:

They give him his orders at Monroe, Virginia,
Sayin' "Petey you're way behind ti-ime"—

"Gosh, it does seem natural to sing when a good horse is putting the miles behind him," said McEwen. "This little old brown pony is holdin' up right well, too, after all that grief in the roughs this mawnin'.

He looked 'round then to his black, greasy fireman,
"Just shovel in a little more co-o-oal,
And when we cross that wide old maounting,
You can watch old Ninety-Seven roll!"

"Hey, Porch Climber! You ain't hardly keepin' time. Peart up a little! Now, lemme see. Must be about twenty mile to the old Wildy Well. Wonder if I'll find any more new ranches between here and there? Likely. Hell of a country, all cluttered up like this!

"It's a mighty rough road from Lynchburg to Danville,
And a line on a three-mile gra-ade;
It was on that grade that he lo-ost his av'rage,
And you see what a jump he made!"[22]

He rejoined the wagon road where the White Sands thrust a long and narrow arm far to the west. The old road crossed this arm at the shoulder, a three-mile speedway. Out on the sands magic islands came and went and rose and sank in a misty sea. But in the south, where the road climbed again to the plain, was the inevitable windmill—reality and no mirage.

McEwen followed the road in the posture of a man who had nothing to fear. He had outridden the rumor of his flight; he could come to this ranch with a good face. But he reined down to a comfortable jog. Those behind might overtake him close enough to spy him here in this naked place. Jaunting easily, nearing the ranch where he belonged, a horseman was no object of suspicion, but a man in haste was a different matter.

There was no one at the ranch. The water was brackish and flat, but the two wayfarers drank thankfully. He could see no signs that any horses were watering there; he made a shrewd guess that the boys had taken the horses and gone up into the mountains for better grass and sweet water, or perhaps to get out of sight of the White Sands, leaving the flats to the cattle.

"Probably they just ride down every so often to oil the windmill," he said. "Leastways, I would. Four hundred square miles of lookin'-glass, three hundred and sixty-four days a year—no, thank you! My eyes are 'most out now."

JB was branded on the gate posts of the corral; JB was branded on the

22 "The Wreck of the Old '97" was a ballad about a train derailment in Virginia in 1903.

door. He found canned stuff on a shelf and a few baking-powder biscuits, old and dry. He took a can of salmon and filed it for future reference.

"No time for gormandizin', now," he said. He stuffed the stale biscuits into his pocket to eat on the road. "There's this much about bread," said McEwen, "I can take it or I can leave it alone. And I've been leaving it alone for several days now."

A pencil and a tablet lay on the table. His gray eyes went suddenly a-dance with impish light. He tore out a page and wrote a few words of counsel and advice:

> Hey, you JB waddies[23]: Look out for a fellow with red hair and gray eyes. Medium-sized man. He robbed the bank at Belen, and they think he came this way. Big reward offered for him. Two thousand, I hear. But I don't know for certain. Send word to the ranches up north. I will tell them as far south as Organ.
>
> Jim Huntley.

He hung this news-letter on a nail above the stove.

"There!" he said. "If them gay jaspers that are after me had any sense a-tall, they'd see it was no use to go any further, and they'd stay right here and rest up. But they won't. They'll say, 'Hey, this is the way he went—here's some more of the same old guff! But how ever did that feller get down here without us finding any tracks? You can see what a jump he made.' I don't want to be ugly," said McEwen, "but I've got to cipher up some way to shake loose from these fellows. I want to go to sleep. Now who in hell is Jim Huntley?"

Time for concealment was past. From now on he must set his hope on speed. He rode down the big road boldly and, for a time, at a brisk pace; he munched the dry biscuits and washed them down with warm and salty water from his canteen.

There was no room for another ranch between here and Wildy's Well.

---

23 cowboys

Wildy's was an old established ranch.[24] It was among the possibilities that he might hit here upon some old acquaintance whose failing sight would not note his passing, and who would give him a fresh horse. He was now needing urge of voice and spur for Porch Climber's lagging feet. It sat in his mind that Wildy was dead. His brows knitted with the effort to remember. Yes, Wildy had been killed by a falling horse. Most likely, though, he would find no one living at the well. Not too bad, the water of Wildy's Well—but they would be in the hills with the good grass.

The brown horse was streaked with salt and sweat; he dragged in the slow sand. Here was a narrow broken country of rushing slopes, pinched between the White Sands and the mountains. The road wound up and down in the crowding brush; the footing was a coarse pebbly sand of broken granite from the crumbling hills. Heat waves rose quivering, the White Sands lifted and shuddered to a blinding shimmer, the dream islands were wavering, shifting and indistinct, astir with rumor. McEwen's eyes were dull for sleep, red rimmed and swollen from glare and alkali dust. The salt water was bitter in his belly. The stubble on his face was gray with powdered dust and furrowed with sweat stains; dust was in his nostrils and his ears, and the taste of dust was in his mouth. Porch Climber plowed heavily. And all at once McEwen felt a sudden distaste for his affair.

He had a searching mind and it was not long before he found a cause. That damn song! Dance music. There were places where people danced, where they would dance tonight. There was a garden in Rutherford—

24 The site of a shootout east of the Jarilla mountains in Otero County, New Mexico, in July 1898 when Garrett and his deputies attempted to arrest Oliver Lee and his allies for the Fountain murders.

CHAPTER V

THERE WAS NO ONE at Wildy's Well, no horses there and no sign that any horses were using there. McEwen drank deep of the cool sweet water. When Porch Climber had his fill, McEwen plunged arms and head into the trough. Horse and man sighed together; their eyes met in comfortable understanding.

"Feller," said McEwen, "it was that salt water, much as anything else, that slowed you up, I reckon. Yuh was sure sluggish. And yuh just ought to see yourself now! Nemmine, that's over." He took down his rope, and cut off a length, the spread of his arms. He untwisted this length to three strands, soaked these strands in the trough, wrung them out and knotted them around his waist. He eyed the cattle that had been watering here. They had retreated to the far side at his coming and were now waiting impatiently. "Been many a long year since I've seen any Durham cattle," said McEwen. "Everybody's got white-face stuff now. Reckon they raise these for El Paso market. No feeder will buy 'em, unless with a heavy cut in the price."

He hobbled over and closed the corral gate. Every bone of him was a separate ache. A faint breeze stirred; the mill sails turned lazily; the gears squeaked a protest. Ross looked up with interest.

"That was right good water," he said. "Guess you've earned a greasing." He climbed the tall tower. Wildy's Well dated from before the steel windmill; this was massive and cumbersome, a wooden tower, and the wheel itself was of wood. After his oiling Ross scanned the north with an anxious eye. There was no dust. South by east, far in the central plain, dim hills swam indeterminate through the heat haze—Las Cornudas and Heuco. South by west, gold and rose, the peaks of the Organs peered from behind the last corner of the San Andrés. He searched the north again. He could see no dust—but he could almost see a dust. He shook his head. "Them guys are real intelligent," he said. "I'm losin' my av'rage." He clambered down with some celerity, and set about what he had to do.

He tied the severed end of his rope to the saddle horn, tightened the cinches, swung into the saddle and shook out a loop. Hugging the fence, the cattle tore madly around the corral in a wild cloud of dust. McEwen rode with them on an inner circle, his eye on a big roan steer, his rope whirling in slow and measured rhythms. For a moment the roan steer darted to the lead; the loop shot out, curled over and tightened on both forefeet; Porch Climber whirled smartly to the left; the steer fell heavily. Ross swung off; as he ran, he tugged at the hogging string around his waist. Porch Climber dragged valiantly, Ross ran down the rope, pounced on the struggling steer, gathered three feet together and tied them with the hogging string. These events were practically simultaneous.

McEwen unsaddled the horse. "I guess you can call it a day," he said. He opened the gate and let the frightened cattle run out. "Here," he said, "is where I make a spoon or spoil a horn." He cut a thong from a saddle string and tied his old plow-handle forty-five so that it should not jolt from the scabbard. He made a tight roll of the folded bridle, that lonely can of salmon and his coat, with his saddle blanket wrapped around all; he tied these worldly goods securely behind the cantle. He uncoupled the cinches and let out the quarter straps to the last hole.

The tied steer threshed his head madly, bellowing wild threats of vengeance. McEwen carried the saddle and placed it at the steer's back, where he lay. He found a short and narrow strip of board, like a batten, under the tower; and with this, as the frantic roan steer heaved and threshed in vain efforts to rise, he poked the front cinch under the struggling body, inches at a time, until at last he could reach over and hook his fingers into the cinch ring. Before he could do this he was forced to tie the free foot to the three that were first tied; it had been kicking with so much fury and determination that the task could not be accomplished. Into the cinch ring he tied the free end of his rope, bringing it up between body and tied feet; he took a double of loose rope around his hips, dug his heels into the sand and pulled manfully every time the steer floundered; and so, at last and painfully, drew the cinch under until the saddle was on the steer's back and approximately where it should be. Then he put in the latigo strap, taking two turns, and tugged at the latigo till the saddle was pulled to its rightful place. At every tug the roan steer let out an agonized bawl. Then he passed the hind cinch behind the steer's hips and under the tail, drawing it up tightly so that the saddle could not slip over the steer's withers during the subsequent proceedings.

McEwen stood up and mopped the muddy sweat from his face; he rubbed his aching back. He filled his canteen at the trough, drank again and washed himself. He rolled a smoke; he lashed the canteen firmly to the saddle forks. Porch Climber was rolling in the sand. McEwen took him by the forelock and led him through the open gate.

"If you should ask me," he said, "this corral is a spot where there is going to be trouble, and no place at all for you." He looked up the north road. Nothing in sight.

He went back to the steer. He hitched up his faded blue overalls, tightened his belt and squinted at the sun; he loosened the last-tied foot and coiled the rope at the saddle horn. Then he eased gingerly into the saddle. The steer made lamentable outcry, twisting his neck in a creditable attempt to hook his tormentor; the free foot lashed out madly. But McEwen flattened himself and crouched safely, with a full inch of margin; the steer was near to hooking his own leg and kicking his own face and he subsided with a groan. McEwen settled himself in the saddle.

"Are ye ready?" said McEwen.

"Oi am!" said McEwen.

"Thin go!" said McEwen, and pulled the hogging string.

The steer lurched sideways to his feet, paused for one second of amazement, and left the ground. He pitched, he plunged, he kicked at the stirrups, he hooked at the rider's legs, he leaped, he ran, bawling his terror and fury to the sky; weaving, lunging, twisting he crashed sidelong into the fence, fell, scrambled up in an instant. The shimmy was not yet invented.

But the roan steer shimmied, and he did it nobly; man and saddle rocked and reeled. Then, for the first time, he saw the open gate and thundered through it, abandoning all thought except flight.

Shaken and battered, McEwen was master. The man was a rider. To use the words of a later day, he was "a little warm, but not at all astonished."[25] Yet he had not come off scot-free. When they crashed into the fence he had pulled up his leg, but had taken an ugly bruise upon the hip. The whole performance, and more particularly the shimmy feature, had been a poor poultice for aching bones. Worse than all, the canteen had been crushed between fence and saddle. The priceless water was lost.

His hand still clutched the hogging string; he had no wish to leave that behind for curious minds to ponder upon. Until his mount slowed from a run to a pounding trot, he made no effort to guide him, the more because the steer's chosen course was not far from the direction in which McEwen wished to go. Wildy's Well lay at the extreme southwestern corner of the White Sands, and McEwen's thought was to turn eastward. He meant to try for Luna's Wells, the old stage station in the middle of the desert, on the road which ran obliquely from Organ to Tularosa. When time was ripe McEwen leaned over and slapped his hat into the steer's face, on the right side, to turn him to the left and to the east.

The first attempt at guidance, and the fourth attempt, brought on new bucking spells. McEwen gave him time between lessons; what he most feared was that the roan would "sull," or balk, refusing to go farther. When the steer stopped, McEwen waited until he went on of his own accord; when his progress led approximately toward McEwen's goal, he was allowed to go his own way unmolested. McEwen was bethorned, dragged through mesquite bushes, raked under branches; his shirt was ribboned and torn. But he had his way at last. With danger, with infinite patience and with good judgment, he forced his refractory mount to the left and ever to the left, and so came at last into a deep trail which led due east. Muttering and grumbling, the steer followed the trail.

---

25 Quoted from "The Elephant's Child" (1902) by the British author Rudyard Kipling (1865–1936).

All this had taken time, but speed had also been a factor. When McEwen felt free to turn his head only a half circle of the windmill fans showed above the brush. Wildy's Well was miles behind them.

"Boys," said McEwen, "if you follow me this time, I'll say you're good!"

The steer scuffed and shambled, taking his own gait; he stopped often to rest, his tongue hung out, foam dripped from his mouth. McEwen did not urge him. The way led now through rotten ground and alkali, now through chalk that powdered and billowed in dust; deep trails, channeled by winds at war. As old trails grew too deep for comfort the stock had made new ones to parallel the old; a hundred paths lay side by side.

McEwen was a hard case. A smother of dust was about him, thirst tormented him, his lips were cracked and bleeding, his eyes sunken, his face fallen in; and weariness folded him like a garment.

"Slate water is the best water," said McEwen.

They came from chalk and brush into a better country; poor indeed, and starved, but the air of it was breathable. The sun was low and the long shadows of the hills reached out into the plain. And now he saw, dead in front, the gleaming vane and sails of a windmill. Only the top—the fans seemed to touch the ground—and yet it was clear to see. McEwen plucked up heart. This was not Luna's. Luna's was far beyond. This was a new one. If it stood in a hollow place—and it did—it could not be far away. Water!

For the first time McEwen urged his mount, gently, and only with the loose and raveled tie string. Once was enough. The roan steer stopped, pawed the ground and proclaimed flat rebellion. For ten minutes, perhaps, McEwen sought to overrule him. It was no use. The roan steer was done. He took down his rope. With a little loop he snared a pawing and rebellious forefoot. He pulled up rope and foot with all his failing strength, and took a quick turn on the saddle horn. The roan made one hop and fell flat-long. McEwen tied three feet, though there was scant need for it. He took off the saddle, carried it to the nearest thicket and raised it, with pain, into the forks of a high soap weed, tucking up latigos and cinches. With pain; McEwen, also, was nearly done.

"My horse gave out on me. I toted my saddle aways, but it was too heavy, and I hung it up so the cows couldn't eat it," he said, in the tone of one who recites a lesson.

He untied the steer, then came back hotfoot to his soapweed, thinking that the roan might be in a fighting humor. But the roan was done. He got unsteadily to his feet, with hanging head and slavering jaws; he waited for a little and moved slowly away.

"Glad he didn't get on the prod," said McEwen. "I sure expected it. That was one tired steer. He sure done me a good turn. Guess I'd better be strollin' into camp."

It was a sorry strolling. A hundred yards—a quarter—a half—a mile. The windmill grew taller; the first night breeze was stirring, he could see the fans whirl in the sun. A hundred yards—a quarter—a mile! An hour was gone. The shadows overtook him, passed him; the hills were suddenly very close and near, notched black against a crimson sky. Thirst tortured him, the windmill beckoned, sunset winds urged him on. He came to the brow of the shallow dip in which the ranch lay, he saw a little corral, a water pen, a long dark house beyond; he climbed into the water pen and plunged his face into the trough.

The windmill groaned and whined with a dismal clank and grinding of dry gears. Yet there was a low smoke over the chimney. How was this? The door stood open. Except for the creaking plaint of the windmill, a dead quiet hung about the place, a hint of something ominous and sinister. Stumbling, bruised and outworn, McEwen came to that low dark door. He heard a choking cough, a child's wailing cry. His foot was on the threshold.

"What's wrong? *Que es?*" he called.

A cracked and feeble voice made an answer that he could not hear. Then a man appeared at the inner door; an old man, a Mexican, clutching at the wall for support.

"*El garrotillo*," said the cracked voice. "The strangler—diphtheria."[26]

"I'm here to help you," said McEwen.

---

26 A highly contagious, often fatal bacterial infection of the respiratory system.

CHAPTER VI

OF WHAT TOOK PLACE that night McEwen had never afterward any clear remembrance, except of the first hour or two. The drone of bees was in his ears, and a whir of wings. He moved in a thin, unreal mist, giddy and light-headed, undone by thirst, weariness, loss of sleep—most of all by alkaline and poisonous dust, deep in his lungs. In the weary time that followed, though he daily fell more and more behind on sleep and rest, he was never so near to utter collapse as on this first interminable night. It remained for him a blurred and distorted vision of the dreadful offices of the sickroom; of sickening odors; of stumbling from bed to bed as one sufferer or another shook with paroxysms of choking.

Of a voice, now far off and now clear, insistent with counsel and question, direction and appeal; of lamplight that waned and flared and dwindled again; of creak and clank and pounding of iron on iron in horrible rhythm, endless, slow, intolerable. That would be the windmill. Yes, but where? And what windmill?

Of terror, and weeping, and a young child that screamed. That woman—why, they had always told him grown people didn't take diphtheria. But she had it, all right. Had it as bad as the two youngsters, too. She was the mother, it seemed. Yes, Florencio[27] had told him that. Too bad

27 Florencio Telles actually lived with his family at the Lost Ranch located eight miles east of White Sands ("Dugout Home of Gene Rhodes a Memorial," *Clovis News-Journal*, December 12, 1940, 1).

for the children to die. . . . But who the devil was Florencio? The windmill turned dismally—clank and rattle and groan.

That was the least one choking now—Felix. Swab out his throat again. Hold the light. Careful. That's it. Burn it up. More cloth, old man. Hold the light this way. There, there, *pobrecito*![28] All right now. . . . Something was lurking in the corners, in the shadows. Must go see. Drive it away. What's that? What say? Make coffee? Sure. Coffee. Good idea. Salty coffee. Windmill pumpin' salt water. Batter and pound and squeal. Round and round. Round and round. Round and round. . . . Tell you what. Goin' to grease that damn windmill. Right now. . . . Huh? What's that? Wait till morning? All right. All ri'. Sure.

His feet were leaden. His arms minded well enough, but his hands were simply wonderful. Surprisin' skillful, those hands. How steady they were to clean membranes from little throats. Clever hands! They could bring water to these people, too, lift them up and hold the cup and not spill a drop. They could sponge off hot little bodies when the children cried out in delirium. Wring out rag, too! Wonnerful hands! Mus' call people's 'tention to these hands sometime. There, there, let me wash you some more with the nice cool water. Now, now—nothing will hurt you. Uncle Happy's goin' to be right here, takin' care of you. Now, now—go to sleep—go-o to sleep!

But his feet were so big, so heavy and so clumsy, and his legs were insubordinate. 'Specially the calves. The calf of each leg, where there had once been good muscles of braided steel, was now filled with sluggish water of inferior quality. That wasn't the worst either. There was a distinct blank place, a vacuum, something like the bead in a spirit level, and it shifted here and there as the water sloshed about. Wonder nobody had ever noticed that.

Must be edgin' on toward morning. Sick people are worst between two and four, they say. And they're all easier now, everyone. Both kids asleep—tossin' about! And now the mother was droppin' off. Yes, sir—she's goin' to sleep. What did the old man call her? Estefanía. Yes—Est'fa'—

He woke with sunlight in his eyes. His arm sprawled before him on a

28 poor little

pine table and his head lay on his arm. He raised up, blinking, and looked around. This was the kitchen, a sorry spectacle. The sick-room lay beyond an open door. He sat by that door, where he could see into the sickroom. They were all asleep. The woman stirred uneasily and threw out an arm. The old man lay huddled on a couch beyond the table.

McEwen stared. The fever had passed and his head was reasonably clear. He frowned, piecing together remembered scraps from the night before. The old man was Florencio Telles, the woman was the wife of his dead son, these were his grandchildren. Felix was one. Forget the other name. They had come back from a trip to El Paso a week ago, or some such matter, and must have brought the contagion with them. First one came down with the strangler, then another. Well poisoned with it, likely. Have to boil the drinking water. This was called Rancho Perdido—the Lost Ranch. Well named. The old fellow spoke good English. McEwen was at home in Spanish, and, from what he remembered of last night, the talk had been carried on in either tongue indifferently. What a night!

He rose and tiptoed out with infinite precaution. The wind was dead. He went to the well and found the oil; he climbed up and drenched the bearings and gears. He was surprised to see how weak he was and how sore; and for the first time in his life he knew the feeling of giddiness and was forced to keep one hand clutched tightly to some support as he moved around the platform—he, Ross McEwen.

When he came back the old man met him with finger on lip. They sat on the warm ground, where they could keep watch upon the sickroom, obliquely, through two doors; just far enough away for quiet speech to be unheard.

"Let them sleep. Every minute of sleep for them is so much coined gold. We won't make a move to wake them. And how is it with you, my son, how is it with you, my son?"

"Fine and fancy. When I came here last night I had a thousand aches, and now I've only got one."

"And that one is all over?"

"That's the place. Never mind me. I'll be all right. How long has this been going on?"

"This is the fifth day for the oldest boy, I think. He came down with it first, Demetrio. We thought it was only a sore throat at first. Maybe six days. I am a little mixed up."

"Should think you would be. Now listen. I know something about diphtheria. Not much, but this for certain. Here's what you've got to do, old man: Quick as they wake up in there, you go to bed and stay in bed. You totter around much more and you're going to die. There's your fortune told, and no charge for it."

"Oh, I'm not bad. I do not cough hard. The strangler never hurts old people much." So he said, but every word was an effort.

"Hell, no, you're not bad. Just a walkin' corpse, tha's all. You get to bed and save your strength. When any two of 'em are chokin' to death at once that'll be time enough for you to hobble out and take one of them off my hands. Do they sleep this long, often?"

"Oh, no. This is the first time. They are always better when morning comes, but they have not all slept at the same time, never before. My daughter, you might say, has not slept at all. It has been grief and anxiety with her as much as the sickness. They will all feel encouraged now, since you've come. If it please God, we'll pull them all through."

"Look here!" said McEwen. "It can't be far to Luna's Well. Can't I catch up a horse and lope over there after while—bring help and send for a doctor?"

"There's no one there. Francisco Luna[29] and Casimiro[30] both have driven their stock to the Guadalupe Mountains, weeks ago. It has been too dry. And no one uses the old road now. All travel goes by the new way, beyond the new railroad."

"I found no one at the western ranches yesterday," said McEwen.

"No. Everyone is in the hills. The drought is too bad. There is no one but you. The nearest help is Alamogordo—thirty-five miles. And if you go there some will surely die before you get back. I have no more strength. I will be flat on my back this day."

---

29 Francisco Luna y Garcia (d. 1908), Sierra County rancher and twice-elected county school superintendent.

30 Casimiro Baca (d. 1914), Socorro County rancher and merchant.

"That's where you belong. I'll be nurse and cook for this family. Got anything to cook?"

"Not much. *Frijoles*, jerky, bacon, flour, a little canned stuff and dried peaches."

McEwen frowned. "It is in my mind they ought to have eggs and milk."

"When the cattle come to water you can shut up a cow and a calf—or two of them—and we can have a little milk tonight. I'll show you which ones. As I told you last night, I turned out the cow I was keeping up, for fear I'd get down and she would die here in the pen."

"Don Florencio, I'm afraid I didn't get all you told me last night," said McEwen thoughtfully. "I was wild as a hawk, I reckon. Thought that windmill would certainly drive me crazy. Fever."

The old man nodded. "I knew, my son. It galled my heart to make demands on you, but there was no remedy. It had to be done. I was at the end of my strength. Little Felix, if not the other, would surely have been dead by now except for the mercy of God which sent you here."

McEwen seemed much struck by this last remark. He cocked his head a little to one side painfully, for his neck was stiff; he pursed his lip and held it between finger and thumb for a moment of meditation.

"So that was it!" he said. "I see! Always heard tell that God moves in a mysterious way His wonders to perform. I'll tell a man He does!"

A scanty breakfast, not without gratitude; a pitiful attempt at redding up the hopeless confusion and disorder. The sick woman's eyes followed McEwen as he worked. A good strangling spell all around, including the old man, then a period of respite. McEwen buckled on his gun and brought a hammer and a lard pail to Florencio's bed.

"If you need me, hammer on this, and I'll come a-running. I'm going out to the corral and shoot some beef tea. You tell me about what milk cows to shut up."

Don Florencio described several milk cows. "Any of them. Not all are in to water any one day. Stock generally come in every other day, because they get better grass at a distance. And my brand is TT—for my son Timoteo, who is dead. You will find the cattle in poor shape, but if you wait awhile you may get a smooth one."

McEwen nodded. "I was thinking that," he said. "I want some flour sacks. I'll hang some of the best up under the platform on the windmill tower, where the flies won't bother it."

They heard a shot later. A long time afterward he came in with a good chunk of meat, and set about preparing beef tea. "I shut up a cow to milk," he said. "A lot of saddle horses came in and I shut them up. Not any too much water in the tank. After while the cattle will begin bawling and milling around if the water's low. That will distress our family. Can't have that. So I'll just harness one onto the sweep of the horse power, slip on a blindfold and let him pump. You tell me which ones will work."

The old man described several horses.

"That's O.K.," said McEwen. "I've got two of them in the pen. Your woodpile is played out. Had to chop down some of your back pen for firewood."

He departed to start the horse power. Later, when beef tea had been served all around, he came over and sat by Florencio's bed.

"You have no drop or grain of medicine of any kind," he said, "and our milk won't be very good when we get it, from the looks of the cows—not for sick people. So, everything being just as it is, I didn't look for brands. I beefed the best one I could find, and hung the hide on the fence. Beef tea, right this very now, may make all the difference with our family. Me, I don't believe there's a man in New Mexico mean enough to make a fuss about it under the circumstances. But if there's any kick, there's the hide and I stand back of it. So that'll be all right. The brand was DW."

"It is my very good friend, Dave Woods, at San Nicolas. That will be all right. Don David is *muy simpático*.[31] Sleep now, my son, sleep a little while you may. It will not be long. You have a hard night before you."

"I'm going up on the rising ground and set a couple of soapweeds afire," said McEwen at dark. "They'll make a big blaze and somebody might take notice. I'll hurry right back. Then I'll light some more about ten o'clock and do it again tomorrow night. Someone will be sure to see it. Just once, they might not think anything. But if they see a light in the same place

---

31 very nice

three or four times, they might look down their nose and scratch their old hard head—a smart man might. Don't you think so?"

"Why, yes," said Florencio; "it's worth trying."

"Those boys are not a bit better than they was. And your daughter is worse. We don't want to miss a bet. Yes, and I'll hold a blanket before the fire and take it away and put it back, over and over. That ought to help people guess that it is a signal. Only—they may guess that it was meant for someone else."

"Try it," said Florencio. "It may work. But I am not sure that our sick people are not holding their own. They are no better, certainly, even with your beef-tea medicine. But we can't expect to see a gain, if there is a gain, for days yet. And so far, they seem worse every night and then better every morning. The sunlight cheers them up at first, and then the day gets hot and they seem worse again. Try your signals, by all means. We need all the help there is. But if you could only guess how much less alone I feel now than before you came, good friend!"

"It must have been plain hell!" said the good friend.

"Isn't there any other one thing we can do?" demanded McEwen the next day, cudgeling his brains. It had been a terrible night. The little lives fluttered up and down; Estefanía was certainly worse; Florencio, though he had but few strangling spells, was very weak—the aftermath of his earlier labors.

"Not one thing. My poor ghost, no man could have done more. There is no more to do."

"But there is!" McEwen fairly sprang up, wearied as he was. "We have every handicap in the world, and only one advantage. And we don't use that one advantage. The sun has a feud with all the damn germs there is; your house is built for shade in this hot country. I'm going to tote all of you out in the sun with your bedding, and keep you there a spell. And while you're there I'll tear out a hole in the south end of your little old adobe wall and let more sunlight in. After the dust settles enough I'll bring you back. Then we'll shovel on a little more coal, and study up something else. And tonight we'll light up our signal fires again. Surely someone will be just fool enough to come out and see what the hell it's all about."

Hours later, after this program had been carried out, McEwen roused from a ten-minute sleep and rubbed his fists in his eyes.

"Are you awake, Don Florencio?" he called softly.

"Yes, my son. What is it?"

"It runs in my mind," said McEwen, "that they burn sulphur in diphtheria cases. Now, if I was to take the powder out of my cartridges and wet it down, let it get partly dry and make a smudge with it—a little at a time—There's sulphur in gunpowder. We'll try that little thing." He was already at work with horseshoe pinchers, twisting out the bullet. He looked up eagerly. "Haven't any tar, have you? To stop holes in your water troughs."

"*Hijo*, you shame me. There is a can of piñon pitch, that I use for my troughs, under the second trough at the upper end. I never once thought of that."

"We're getting better every day," said McEwen joyfully. "We'll make a smoke with some of that piñon wax, and we'll steep some of it in boiling water and breathe the steam of it; we'll burn my wet powder, and when that's done, we'll think of something else; and we'll make old bones yet, every damn one of us! By gollies, tomorrow between times I'm goin' to take your little old rifle and shoot some quail."

"Between times? Oh, Happy!"

"Oh, well, you know what I mean—just shovel on a little more coal—better brag than whine. Hi, Estefanía—hear that? We've dug up some medicine. Yes, we have. Ask Don Florencio if we haven't. I'm going after it."

But as he limped past the window on his way to the corral he heard the sound of a sob. He paused midstep, thinking it was little Felix. But it was Estefanía.

"*Madre de Dios, ayudale su enviado!*"[32] He tiptoed away, shamefaced.

---

32 "Mother of God, help your messenger!"

CHAPTER VII

SLEEPING ON A VERY thin bed behind a very large boulder, two men camped at the pass of San Agustin; a tall young man and a taller man who was not so young. The very tall man was Pat Garrett, sheriff of Doña Ana, sometime sheriff of other counties. The younger man was Clint Llewellyn,[33] his deputy, and their camp was official in character. They were keeping an eye out for that Belen bandit, after prolonged search elsewhere.

"Not but what he's got away long ago," said Pat, in his quiet drawling speech, "but just in case he might possibly double back this way."

It was near ten at night when Pat saw the light on the desert. He pointed it out to Clint. "See that fire out there? Your eyes are younger than mine. Isn't it sinking down and then flaring up again?"

"Looks like it is," said Clint. "I saw a fire there—or two of 'em, rather—just about dark, while you took the horses down to water."

"Did you?" said Pat. He stroked his mustache with a large slow hand. "Looks to me like someone was trying to attract attention."

"It does, at that," said Clint. "Don't suppose somebody's had a horse fall with him and got smashed, do you?"

"Do you know," said Pat slowly, "that idea makes me ache, sort of? One thing pretty clear. Somebody wants someone to do something for

---

33 Clint Llewellyn (1877–1903), one of Garrett's deputies and member of the posse charged with arresting Oliver Lee in 1898.

somebody. Reckon that's us. Looks like a long ride, and maybe for nothing. Yes. But then we're two long men. Where do you place that fire, Clint?"

"Hard to tell. Close to Luna's Wells, maybe."

"Too far west for that," said Garrett. "I'd say it was Lost Ranch. We'll go ask questions anyway. If we was layin' out there with our ribs caved in or our leg broke—Let's go!"

That is how they came to Lost Ranch between three and four the next morning. A feeble light shone in the window. Clint took the horses to water, while Garrett went on to the house. He stopped at the outer door. A man lay on a couch within, a man Garrett knew—old Florencio. Folded quilts made a pallet on the floor, and on the quilts lay another man, a man with red hair and a red stubble of beard. Both were asleep. Florencio's hand hung over the couch, and the stranger's hand held to it in a tight straining clasp. Garrett stroked his chin, frowning.

Sudden and startling, a burst of strangled coughing came from the room beyond and a woman's sharp call.

"*Hijo!*" cried Florencio feebly, and pulled the hand he held. "Happy! Wake up!" The stranger lurched to his feet and staggered through the door. "Yes, Felix, I'm coming. All right, boy! All right now! Let me see. It won't hurt. Just a minute, now."

Garrett went into the house.

"Clint," said Pat Garrett, "there's folks dyin' in there, and a dead man doin' for them. You take both horses and light a rag for the Alamogordo Hospital. Diphtheria. Get a doctor and nurses out here just as quick as God will let them come." Garrett was pulling the saddle from his horse as he spoke. "Have 'em bring grub and everything. Ridin' turn about, you ought to make it tolerable quick. I'm stayin' here, but there's no use of your comin' back. You might take a look around Jarilla if you want to, but use your own judgment. Drag it, now. Every minute counts."

A specter came to the doorway. "Better send a wagonload of water," it said as Clint turned to go. "This well is maybe poisoned. Germs and such."

"Yes, and bedding, too," said Clint. "I'll get everything and tobacco. So long!"

“Friend,” said Pat, “you get yourself to bed. I’m takin’ on your job. Your part is to sleep.”

“Yes, son,” Florencio’s thin voice quavered joyously. “*Duerme y descansa.* Sleep and rest. Don Patricio will do everything.”

McEwen swayed uncertainly. He looked at Garrett with stupid and heavy eyes. “He called you Patricio. You’re not Pat Nunn,[34] by any chance?”

“Why not?” said Garrett.

McEwen’s voice was lifeless. “My father used to know you,” he said drowsily. He slumped over on his bed.

“Who was your father?” said Garrett.

McEwen’s dull and glassy eyes opened to look at his questioner.

“I’m no credit to him,” he said. His eyes closed again. “Boil the water!” said McEwen.

“He’s asleep already!” said Pat Garrett. “The man’s dead on his feet.”

“Oh, Pat, there was never one like him!” said Florencio. He struggled to his elbow, and looked down with pride and affection at the sprawling shape on the pallet. “Don Patricio, I have a son in my old age, like Abrahán!”[35]

“I’ll pull off his boots,” said Pat Garrett.

Garrett knelt over McEwen and shook him vigorously. “Hey, fellow, wake up! You, Happy—come alive! Snap out of it! Most sundown, and time you undressed and went to bed.”

McEwen set up at last, rubbing his eyes. He looked at the big, kindly face for a little in some puzzlement. Then he nodded.

“I remember you now. You sent your pardner for the doctor. How’s the sick folks?”

“I do believe,” said Pat, “that we’re going to pull ’em through—everyone. You sure had a tough lay.”

“Yes. Doctor come?”

---

34 Pat Nunn (1878–1916), former manager of the Diamond A ranch near Lordsburg, New Mexico.

35 Abrahán = Abraham

"He's in sight now—him and the nurses. That's how come me to rouse you up. Fellow, I hated to wake you when you was going so good. But with the ladies comin', you want to spruce yourself up a bit. You look like the wrath of God!"

McEwen got painfully to his feet and wriggled his arms experimentally.

"I'm just one big ache," he admitted. "Who's them fellows?" he demanded. Two men were industriously cleaning up the house; two men that he had never seen.

"Them boys? Monte, the Mexican, he's old Florencio's nephew. Heard the news this mawnin', and comes boilin' out here hell-for-leather. Been here for hours. The other young fellow came with him. Eastern lad. Don't know him, or why he came. Say, Mr. Happy, you want to bathe those two eyes of yours with cold water, or hot water, or both. They look like two holes burned in a blanket. Doc will have to give you a good jolt of whisky too. Man, you're pretty nigh ruined!"

"I knew there was something," said Mr. Happy. "Got to get me a name. And gosh, I'm tired! I'm a good plausible liar, most times, but I'll have to ask you to help out. Andy Hightower—how'd that do? Knew a man named Alan Hightower[36] once, over on the Mangas."

"Does he run cattle over there now somewhere about Quemado?"

"Yes," said McEwen.

"I wouldn't advise Hightower," said Garrett.

"My name," said McEwen, "is Henry Clay."[37]

Doctor Lamb, himself the driver of the covered spring wagon, reached Lost Ranch at sundown. He brought with him two nurses, Miss Mason and Miss Jay Hollister, with Lida Hopper, who was to be cook; also, many

---

36 Rhodes jokes about his friend Clemente Hightower (1857–1931), a cowboy who drove cattle along the Rio Grande in 1877, newspaper editor, and New Mexico politician ("Hightower and Rhodes Describe Days of Old," *Santa Fe New Mexican*, March 1, 1927, 2; "Hightower to Assist Gene Rhodes in His New Mexico History," *Santa Fe New Mexican*, April 16, 1928, 4).

37 The American statesman Henry Clay (1777–1852) was nicknamed "the Great Compromiser." Rhodes also gave the name to one of his cats (May Rhodes, 171).

hampers and much bedding. Dad Lucas[38] was coming behind, the doctor explained, with a heavy wagon loaded with water and necessaries. Garrett led the way to the sick-room.

Monte helped Garrett unload the wagon and care for the team; Lida Hopper prepared supper in the kitchen.

Mr. Clay had discreetly withdrawn, together with the other man. They were out in the corral now, getting acquainted. The other man, it may be mentioned, was none other than Ben Griggs; and his discretion was such that Miss Hollister knew nothing of his presence until the next morning.

Mr. Clay, still wearied, bedded down under the stars, Monte rustling the credentials for him. When Dad Lucas rolled in, the men made camp by the wagon.

"Well, doctor," said Garrett, "how about the sick? They going to make it?"

"I think the chances are excellent," said the doctor. "Barring relapse, we should save everyone. But it was a narrow squeak. That young man who nursed them through—why, Mr. Garrett, no one on earth could have done better, considering what he had to do with. Nothing, practically, but his two hands."

"You're all wrong there, doc. He had a backbone all the way from his neck to the seat of his pants. That man," said Garrett, "will do to take along."

"Where is he, Mr. Garrett? And what's his name? The old man calls him 'son,' all the boys call him 'Uncle Happy.' What's his right name?"

"Clay," said Garrett. "He's dead to the world. You won't see much of him. A week of sleep is what he needs. But you remind me of something. If you will allow it I would like to speak to all of you together. Just a second. Would you mind asking the nurses to step in for a minute or two, while I bring the cook?"

"Certainly," said Doctor Lamb.

"I want to ask a favor of all of you," said Garrett, when the doctor had

38 The rancher "Uncle George" Lucas (1863–1936) settled in Eddy County, New Mexico, in 1879.

ushered in the nurses. "I won't keep you. I just want to declare myself. Some of you know me, and some don't. My name is Pat Garrett, and I am the sheriff of Doña Ana County, over west. But for reasons that are entirely satisfactory to myself, I would like to be known as Pat Nunn, for the present. That's all. I thank you."

"Of course," said Doctor Lamb, "if it is to serve the purpose of the law—"

"I would not go so far," said Garrett. "If you put it that my purpose is served, you will be quite within the truth. Besides, this is not official. I am not sheriff here. This ranch is just cleverly over the line and in Otero County. Old Florencio pays taxes in Otero. I am asking this as a personal favor, and only for a few days. Perfectly simple. That's all. Thank you."

"Did you ask the men outside?"

"No. I just told them," said Mr. Pat Nunn. "It would be dishonorable for a lady to tip my hand; for a man it would be plumb indiscreet."

"Dad Lucas," said the doctor, "is a cynical old scoundrel, and a man without principle, and swivel tongued besides."

"He is all that you say, and a lot more that you would never guess," said Garrett, "but if I claimed to be Humpty Dumpty, Dad Lucas would swear that he saw me fall off of the wall." He held up his two index fingers, side by side. "Dad and me, we're like that. We've seen trouble together—and there is no bond so close. Again, one and all, I thank you. Meetin's adjourned."

Lost Ranch was a busy scene on the following day. A cheerful scene, too, despite the blazing sun, the parched desert and the scarred old house. Reports from the sick-room were hopeful. The men had spread a tarpaulin by the wagon, electing Dad Lucas for cook. They had salvaged a razor of Florencio's and were now doing mightily with it. Monte and Ben Griggs, after dinner, were to take Dad's team and Florencio's wagon to draw up a jag of mesquite roots. In the meantime Monte dragged up stop-gap firewood by the saddle horn, and Ben kept the horse power running in the water pen. Keeping him company, Pat Garrett washed Henry Clay's clothes. More accurately, it was Pat Nunn who did this needed work with grave and conscientious thoroughness.

"Henry Clay and me, after bein' in the house so long," said Mr. Nunn, "why, we'll have to boil up our clothes before we leave, or we might go scattering diphtheria hither and yonder and elsewhere."

"But how if you take it yourselves?"

"Then we'll either die or get well," said Mr. Nunn slowly. "In either case, things will keep juneing along just the same. Henry Clay ain't going to take it, or he'd have it now. It takes three days after you're exposed. Something like that. We'll stick around a little before we go, just in case."

"Which way are you going, Mr. Nunn?" asked Ben.

"Well, I'm going to Tularosa. Old Florencio will have to loan me a horse. Clay too. He's afoot. Don't know where he's going. Haven't asked him. He's too worn out to talk much. His horse played out on him out on the flat somewheres and he had to hang up his saddle and walk in. So Florencio told me. He's goin' back and get his saddle tomorrow."

Miss Mason being on duty, Jay Hollister, having picked up a bite of breakfast, was minded to get a breath of fresh air; and at this juncture she tripped into the water pen where Mr. Nunn and Ben plied their labors.

"And how is the workingman's bride this morning?" asked Ben brightly.

"Great Cæsar's ghost! Ben Griggs, what in the world are you doing here?" demanded Jay with a heightened color.

"Workin'," said Ben, and fingered his blue overalls proudly. "Told you I was goin' to work. Right here is where I'm needed. Why, there are only four of us, not counting you three girls and the doctor, to do what Clay was doing. You should have seen Monte and me cleaning house yesterday."

"Yes?" Jay smiled sweetly. "What house was that?"

"Woman!" said Ben, touched in his workman's pride. "If you feel that way now, you should have seen this house when we got here."

"You're part fool. You'll catch diphtheria."

"Well, what about you? The diphtheria part, I mean. What's the matter with your gettin' diphtheria?"

"That's different. That's a trade risk. That's my business."

"You're my business," said Ben.

Jay shot a startled glance at Mr. Nunn, and shook her head.

"Oh, yes!" said Ben. "Young woman, have you met Mr. Nunn?"

Soap in hand, Mr. Nunn looked up from his task. "Good morning, miss. Don't mind me," he said. "Go right on with the butchery."

"Good morning, Mr. Nunn. Please excuse us. I was startled at finding this poor simpleton out here where he has no business to be. Have I met Mr. Nunn? Oh, yes, I've met him twice. The doctor introduced him once, and he introduced himself once."

Mr. Nunn acknowledged this gibe with twinkling eye. Miss Hollister looked around her, and shivered in the sun. "What a ghastly place!" she cried. "I can't for the life of me understand why anybody should live here. We came through some horrible country yesterday, but this is the worst yet. Honestly, Mr. Nunn, isn't this absolutely the most God-forsaken spot on earth?"

Mr. Nunn abandoned his work for the moment and stood up, smiling. So this was Pat Garrett of whom she had heard so much; the man who killed Billy the Kid. Well, he had a way with him. Jay could not but admire the big square head, the broad spread of his shoulders and a certain untroubled serenity in his quiet face.

"Oh, I don't know," said Mr. Nunn. "Look there!"

"Where? I don't see anything," said Jay. "Look at what?"

"Why, the bees," said Pat. "The wild bees. They make honey here. Little family of 'em in every *sotol* stalk; and that old house up there with the end broken in—No, Miss Hollister, I've seen worse places than this."

CHAPTER VIII

THE PATIENTS WERE IMPROVING. Old Florencio, who had been but lightly touched, mended apace. He had suffered from exhaustion and distress quite as much as from disease itself. Demetrio and little Felix gained more slowly, and Estefanía was weakest of all. The last was contrary to expectation. As a usual thing, diphtheria goes hardest with the young. But all were in a fair way to recover. Doctor Lamb and Dad Lucas had gone back to town. Dad had returned with certain comforts and luxuries for the convalescents.

Jay Hollister, on the morning watch, was slightly annoyed. Mr. Pat Garrett and the man Clay were leaving, it seemed, and nothing would do but that Clay must come to the sick-room for leave-taking. Quite naturally, Jay had not wished her charges disturbed. Peace and quiet were what they needed. But Garrett had been insistent, and he had a way with him. Oh, well! The farewell was quiet enough and brief enough on Clay's part, goodness knows, but rather fervent from old Florencio and his daughter-in-law. That was the Spanish of it, Jay supposed. Anyhow, that was all over and the disturbers were on their way to Tularosa.

Relieved by Miss Mason, Jay went in search of Ben Griggs to impart her grievance, conscious that she would get no sympathy there, and queerly unresentful of that lack. He was not to be seen. She went to the kitchen.

"Where's that trifling Ben, Lida?"

"Him? I'm sure I don't know, Miss Jay. That Mexican went up on top of the house just now. He'll know, likely."

Jay climbed the rickety ladder, stepped on the adobe parapet and so down to the flat roof. Monte sat on the farther wall, looking out across the plain so intently that he did not hear her coming.

"Do you know where Ben is?" said Jay.

Monte came to his feet. "Oh, yais! He is weeth the Señor Lucas to haul wood, Mees Hollister. Is there what I can do?"

"What are we going to do about water?" said Jay. "There's only one barrel left. Of course we can boil the well water, but it's horrible stuff."

"*Prontamente*—queekly. All set. Ben weel be soon back, and here we go, Ben and me, to the spreeng of San Nicolás." He pointed to a granite peak of the San Andrés. "There at thees peenk hill yonder."

"What, from way over there?"

"Eet ees closest, an ver' sweet water, ver' good."

Jay looked and wondered, tried to estimate the void that lay between, and could not even guess. "What a dreadful country! How far is it?"

"Oh, twent-ee miles. *Es nada.*[39] We feel up by sundown and come back in the cool stars."

"Oh, do sit down," said Jay, "and put on your hat. You're so polite you make me nervous. I shouldn't think you'd care much about the cool," said Jay, "the way you sit up here, for pleasure, in the broiling sun."

"Plezzer? Oh, no!" said Monte. "Look!" He turned and pointed. "No, not here, not close by. Mebbe four, three miles. Look across thees bare spot an' thees streep of mesquite to thees long chalk reedge; and now, beyond thees row and bunches of yuccas. You see them now?"

Jay followed his hand and saw, small and remote, two horsemen creeping black and small against the infinite recession of desert. She nodded.

"Eet ees with no joy," said Monte, "that I am to see the las' of *un caballero valiente*—how do you say heem?—of a gallan' gentleman—thees redhead."

"You are not very complimentary to Mr. Garrett," said Jay.

"Oh, no, no, no—you do not unnerstand! " Monte's eyes narrowed with both pity and puzzlement. He groped visibly for words. "*Seguramente,*

39 It's nothing.

siempre,[40] een all ways Pat Garrett ees a man complete. Eet is known. But thees young fellow—he ees play out the streeng—*pobrecito*! Oh, Mees Jay, eet ees a bad spread! Es-scusame, please, Mees Hollister. I have not the good words—onlee the man talk."

"Oh, he did well enough—but why not?" said Jay. "What else could he do? There has been something all the time that I don't understand. Danger from diphtheria? Nonsense. I am not a bit partial to you people out here. Perhaps you know that. But I must admit that danger doesn't turn you from anything you have set your silly heads to do. Of course Mr. Clay had to work uncommonly hard, all alone here. But he had no choice. No; it's something else, something you have kept hidden from me all along. Why all the conspiracy and the pussyfoot mystery?"

"Eet was not jus' lak that, mees. Not *conjuration*[41] exactlee. But everee man feel for heemself eet ees ver' good to mek no talk of thees theeng." For once Monte's hands were still. He looked off silently at the great bare plain and the little horsemen dwindling in the distance. "I weel tell you, then," he said at last. "Thees *cosa*[42] are bes' not spoken, and yet eet ees right for you shall know. Onlee I have not those right words. Ben, he shall tell you when he come."

Again he held silence for a little space, considering. "Eet ees lak thees, Mees Jay. Ver' long ago—yais, before not any of your people is cross over the Atlantic Ocean—my people they are here een thees country and they go up and down to all places—yais, to *las playas de mar*,[43] to the shores of the sea by California. And when they go by Zuñi and by thees rock El Morro, wheech your people call—I have forget that name. You have heard heem?"

"Yes," said Jay. "Inscription Rock.[44] I've read about it."

---

40 Certainly, always

41 conspiracy

42 matters

43 sea beaches

44 The carvings, mostly of names in Inscription Rock at El Morro National Monument in Cibola County, New Mexico, date back to the Spanish conquistadors of the early-seventeenth century.

"*Si, si!* That ees the name. Well, eet ees good campground, El Morro, wood and water, and thees gr-reat cleef for shade and for shelter een estr-rong winds. And here some fellow he come and he cry out, '*Adiós, el mundo!*'[45] What lar-rge weelderness ees thees! And me, I go now eento thees beeg lonesome, and perhaps I shall not to r-return! *Bueno, pues*,[46] I mek now for me a gravestone!' And so he mek on that beeg rock weeth hees dagger, *Pasó por aquí, Don Fulano de Tal*[47]—passed by here, Meester So-and-So—weeth the year of eet. And after heem come others to El Morro—so few, so far from Spain! They see what he ees write there, and they say, '*Con razón*!'[48]—eet ees weeth reason to do thees. An' they also mek eenscreepción, *Pasó por aquí*—and their names, and the year of eet."

His hand carved slow letters in the air. His eye was proud. "I would not push my leetleness upon thees so lar-rge world, but one of thees, Mees Hollister—oh, not of the great, not of the first—he was of mine, my ver' great, great papa. So long ago! And he mek also '*Pasó por aquí*, Salvador Holguín.'[49] I hear thees een the firelight when I am small fellow. And when I am man-high I mek veesit to thees place and see heem."

His eyes followed the far horsemen, now barely to be seen, a faint moving blur along the north.

"And thees fellow, too, thees redhead, he pass this way, '*Pasó por aquí*'"—again the brown hand wrote in the air—"and he mek here good and not weeked. But, before that—I am not God!" Lips, shoulders, hands, every line of his face disclaimed that responsibility. "But he is thief, I theenk," said Monte. "Yais, he ees thees one—Mack-Yune?—who rob the bank of Numa Frenger las' week at Belen. I theenk so."

Jay's eyes grew round with horror, her hand went to her throat. "Not arrested?"

---

45 Good-bye, world.

46 Well, then.

47 Mr. So-and-So

48 justly

49 The Holguín or Olguín family of Rio Arriba County, New Mexico, traces its lineage to the seventeenth century and its ancestor Salvador Holguín (1637–1693), an officer in Juan de Oñate y Salazar's army.

For once Monte's serene composure was shaken. His eyes narrowed, his words came headlong.

"Oh, no, no, no! You do not unnerstan'. Ees eemposevilly, what you say! Pat Garrett ees know nozzing, he ees fir-rm r-resolve to know nozzing. An' thees Mack-Yune, he ees theenk *por verdad* eet ees Pat Nunn who ride weeth heem to Tularosa. He guess not one theeng that eet ees the sheriff. Pat Garrett he go that none may deesturb or moless' heem. Becows, thees young fellow ees tek eshame for thees bad life, an' he say to heemself, 'I weel arize and go to my papa.'"[50]

She began to understand. She looked out across the desert and the thorn, the white chalk and the sand. Sun dazzle was in her eyes. These people! Peasant, gambler, killer, thief—She felt the pulse pound in her throat.

"And een Tularosa, all old-timers, everee man he know Pat Garrett. Not lak thees Alamogordo, new peoples. And when thees old ones een Tularosa see Meester Pat Garrett mek good-by weeth hees friend at the tr-rain, they will theenk nozzing, say nozzing. *Adiós.*" He sat sidewise upon the parapet and waved his hand to the nothingness where the two horsemen had been swallowed up at last.

"And him the sheriff!" said Jay. "Why, they could impeach him for that. They could throw him out of office."

He looked up, smiling. "But who weel tell?" said Monte. His outspread hands were triumphant. "We are all decent people."

"Yes, Monte," said Jay. Her hand reached out to touch his shoulder. "Clean people." She turned and flung out her arms to earth and sky.

"The beautiful world!" said Jay.

---

50 A paraphrase of the words of the prodigal son in Luke 15:18.

The Desire of the Moth

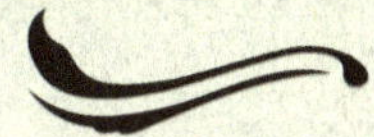

CHAPTER I

Little Next Door—her years are few—
Loves me, more than her elders do;
Says, my wrinkles become me so;
Marvels much at the tales I know.
Says, we shall marry when she is grown—[1]

The little happy song stopped short. John Wesley Pringle, at the mesa's last headland, drew rein to adjust his geography. This was new country to him.

Close behind, Organ Mountain flung up a fantasy of spires, needle-sharp and bare and golden. The long straight range—saw-toothed limestone save for this twenty-mile sheer upheaval of the Organ—stretched away to north and south against the unclouded sky, till distance turned the barren gray to blue-black, to blue, to misty haze; till the sharp, square-angled masses rounded to hillocks—to a blur—a wavy line—nothing.

More than a hundred miles to the northwest, two midget mountains wavered in the sky. John Wesley nodded at their unforgotten shapes and pieced this vast landscape to the patchwork map in his head. Those toy hills were San Mateo and Magdalena. Pringle had passed that way on a bygone year, headed east. He was going west, now.

1 Rhodes' poem "Little Next Door" is published in its entirety in *Out West* 43 (January 1916), 4.

"I'm too prosperous here," he had explained to Beebe[2] and Ballinger,[3] his partners on Rainbow. "I'm tedious to myself. Guess I'll take a *pasear* back to Prescott. Railroad? Who, me? Why, son, I like to travel when I go anywheres. Just starting and arriving don't delight me any. Besides, I don't know that strip along the border. I'll ride."

It was a tidy step to Prescott—say, as far as from Philadelphia to Savannah, or from Richmond to Augusta; but John Wesley had made many such rides in the Odyssey of his wonder years. Some of them had been made in haste. But there was no haste now. Sam Bass,[4] his corn-fed sorrel, was hardly less sleek and sturdy than at the start, though a third of the way was behind him. Pringle rode by easy stages, and where he found himself pleased, there he tarried for a space.

With another friendly nod to the northward hills that marked a day of his past, Pringle turned his eyes to the westlands, outspread and vast before him. To his right the desert stretched away, a mighty plain dotted with low hills, rimmed with a curving, jagged range. Beyond that range was a nothingness, a hiatus that marked the sunken valley of the Rio Grande; beyond that, a headlong infinity of unknown ranges, tier on tier, yellow or brown or blue; broken, tumbled, huddled, scattered, with gulfs between to tell of unseen plains and hidden happy valleys—altogether giving an impression of rushing toward him, resistless, like the waves of a stormy sea.

At his feet the plain broke away sharply, in a series of steplike sandy benches, to where the Rio Grande bore quartering across the desert, turning to the Mexican sea; the Mesilla Valley here, a slender ribbon of mossy green, broidered with loops of flashing river—a ribbon six miles by forty, orchard, woodland, and green field, greener for the desolate gray desert beyond and the yellow hills of sand edging the valley floor. Below him Las Uvas, chief town of the valley, lay basking in the sun, tiny square and street bordered with greenery: its domino houses white-walled in the sun, with larger splashes of red from courthouse or church or school.

---

2 The cowboy William D. "Bill" Barbee (1853–1926) was Rhodes' friend in early life.

3 C. C. Ballinger, a rancher near Berino in Doña Ana County.

4 Sam Bass (1851–1878), a notorious Texas outlaw.

Far on the westering desert, beyond the valley, Pringle saw a white feather of smoke from a toiling train; beyond that a twisting gap in the blue of the westmost range.

"That's our road." He lifted his bridle rein. "Amble along, Sam!"

To that amble he crooned to himself, pleasantly, half-dreamily—as if he voiced indirectly some inner thought—quaint snatches of old song:

She came to the gate and she peeped in—
Grass and the weeds up to her chin;
Said, "A rake and a hoe and a fantail plow
Would suit you better than a wife just now."[5]

And again:

Schooldays are over now,
Lost all our bliss;
But love remembers yet
Quarrel and kiss.
Still, as in days of yore—[6]

Then, after a long silence, with a thoughtful earnestness that Rainbow would scarce have credited, he quoted a verse from what he was wont to call Billy Beebe's Bible:

One Moment in Annihilation's waste,
One Moment of the Well of Life to taste—
The Stars are setting, and the Caravan
Starts for the Dawn of—Nothing. Oh, make haste![7]

---

5 Rhodes' original verse.

6 Rhodes' original verse.

7 The first line of the first quatrain in section 38 of Edward FitzGerald's English translation of the *Rubáiyát of Omar Khayyam.*

After late dinner at the Gadsden Purchase,[8] Pringle had tidings of the Motion Picture Palace[9]; and thither he bent his steps. He was late and the palace was a very small palace indeed; it was with difficulty that he spied in the semidarkness an empty seat in a side section. A fat lady and a fatter man, in the seats nearest the aisle, obligingly moved over rather than risk any attempt to squeeze by.

Beyond them, as he took the end seat, Pringle was dimly aware of a girl who looked at him rather attentively.

He turned his mind to the screen, where a natty and noble young man, with a chin, bit off his words distinctly and smote his extended palm with folded gloves to emphasize the remarks he was making to a far less natty man with black mustaches. John Wesley rightly concluded that this second man, who gnashed his teeth so convincingly, and at whom an incredibly beautiful young lady looked with haughty disdain, was the villain, and foiled.

The blond and shaven hero, with a magnificent gesture, motioned the villain to begone! That baffled person, after waiting long enough to register despair, spread his fingers across his brow and be–went; the hero turned, held out his arms; the scornful young beauty crept into them. Click! On the screen appeared a scroll:

Keep Your Seats. Two Minutes to Change Reels.

The lights were turned on. Pringle looked at the crowd—girls, grandmas, mothers with their families, many boys, and few men; Americans, Mexicans, well-dressed folk and roughly dressed, all together. Many were leaving; among them Pringle's fat and obliging neighbors rose with a pleasant: "Excuse me, please!"

A stream of newcomers trickled in through the door. As Pringle sat down the lights were dimmed again. Simultaneously the girl he had noticed beyond the fat couple moved over to the seat next to his own. Pringle did not look at her; and a little later he felt a hand on his sleeve.

---

8 A fictional restaurant named for the territory in present-day southwestern New Mexico and southern Arizona the United States bought from Mexico in 1854.

9 The Fountain Theatre in Old Mesilla near Las Cruces, built in 1905 and the oldest motion picture theater in New Mexico, seats only about a hundred.

"Tut, tut!" said Pringle in a tolerant undertone. "Why, chicken, you're not trying to get gay with your old Uncle Dudley, are you?"

"John Wesley Pringle!" came the answer in a furious whisper, each indignant word a missile. "How dare you! How dare you speak to me like that?"

"What!" said Pringle, peering. "What! Stella Vorhis! I can hardly believe it!"

"But it's oh-so-true!" said Stella, rising. "Let's go—we can't talk here."

"That was one awful break I made. I most sincerely and humbly beg your pardon," Pringle said on the sidewalk.

Stella laughed.

"That's all right—I understand—forget it! You hadn't looked at me. But I knew you when you first came in—only I wasn't sure till the lights were turned on. Of course it would be great fun to tease you—pretend to be shocked and dreadfully angry, and all that—but I haven't got time. And oh, John Wesley, I'm so delighted to see you again! Let's go over to the park. Not but what I was dreadfully angry, sure enough, until I had a second to think. Why don't you say you're glad to see me—after five years?"

"Stella! You know I am. Six years, please. But I thought you were still in Prescott?"

"We came here three years ago. Here's a bench. Now tell it to me!"

But Pringle stood beside and looked down at her without speech, with a smile unexpected from a face so lean, so brown, so year-bitten and iron-hard—a smile which happily changed that face, and softened it.

The girl's eyes danced at him.

"I'm so glad you've come, John Wesley! Good old Wes!"

"So I am—both those little things. Six years!" he said slowly. "Dear me—dear both of us! That will make you twenty-five. You don't look a day over twenty-four! But you're still Stella Vorhis?"

She met his gaze gravely; then her lids drooped and a wave of red flushed her face.

"I am Stella Vorhis—yet."

"Meaning—for a little while yet?"

"Meaning, for a little while yet. That will come later, John Wesley. Oh, I'll tell you, but not just now. You tell about John Wesley, first—and remember, anything you say may be used against you. Where have you been? Were you dead? Why didn't you write? Has the world used you well? Sit down, Mr. John Wesley Also-Ran Pringle, and give an account of yourself!"

He sat beside her: she laid her hand across his gnarled brown fingers with an unconscious caress.

"It's good to see you, old-timer! Begin now—I, John Wesley Pringle, am come from going to and fro upon the earth and from walking up and down in it. But I didn't ask you where you were living. Perhaps you have a—home of your own now."

John Wesley firmly lifted her slim fingers from his hand and as firmly deposited them in her lap.

"Kindly keep your hands to yourself, young woman," he said with stately dignity. "Here is an exact account of all my time since I saw you: I have been hungry, thirsty, sleepy, tired. To remedy these evils, upon expert advice I have eaten, drunk, slept, and rested. I have worked and played, been dull and gay, busy and idle, foolish and unwise. That's all. Oh, yes— I'm living in Rainbow Mountain; cattle. Two pardners—nice boys but educated. Had another one; he's married now, poor dear—and just as happy as if he had some sense."

"You're not?"

"Not what—happy or married?"

"Married, silly!"

"And I'm not. Now it's your turn. Where do you live? Here in town?"

"Oh, no. Dad's got a farm twenty miles up the river and a ranch out on the flat. I just came down on the morning train to do a little shopping and go back on the four-forty-eight—and I'll have to be starting soon. You'll walk down to the station with me?"

"But the sad story of your life?" objected Pringle.

"Oh, I'll tell you that by installments. You're to make us a long, long visit, you know—just as long as you can stay. You're horseback, of course? Well, then, ride up to-night. Ask for Aden Station. We live just beyond there."

"But the Major was a very hostile major when I saw him last."

"Oh, father's got all over that. He hadn't heard your side of it then. He often speaks of you now and he'll be glad to see you."

"To-morrow, then. My horse is tired—I'll stay here to-night."

"You'll find dad changed," said the girl. "This is the first time in his life he has ever been at ease about money matters. He's really quite well-to-do."

"That's good. I'm doing well in that line too. I forgot to tell you." There was no elation in his voice; he looked back with a pang to the bold and splendid years of their poverty. "Then the Major will quit wandering round like a lost cat, won't he?"

"I think he likes it here—only for the crazy-mad political feeling; and I think he's settled down for good."

"High time, I think, at his age."

"You needn't talk! Dad's only ten years older than you are." She leaned her cheek on her hand, she brushed back a little stray tendril of midnight hair from her dark eyes, and considered him thoughtfully. "Why, John Wesley, I've known you nearly all my life and you don't look much older now than when I first saw you."

"That was in Virginia City. You were just six years old and your pony ran away with you. We were great old chums for a month or so. The next time I saw you was—"

"At Bakersfield—at mother's funeral," said the girl softly. "Then you came to Prescott, and you had lost your thumb in the meantime; and I was Little Next Door to you—"

"And Prescott and me, we agreed it was best for both of us that I should go away."

"Yes; and when you came back you were going to stay. Why didn't you stay, John Wesley?"

"I think," said Pringle reflectively, "that I have forgotten that."

"Do you know, John Wesley, I have never been back to any place we have left once? And of all the people I have ever known, you are the only one I have ever lost track of and found again. And you're always just the same old John Wesley; always gay and cheerful; nearly always in trouble; always strong and resourceful—"

"How true!" said Pringle. "Yes, yes; go on!"

"Well, you are! And you're so—so reliable; like Faithful John in the fairy story.[10] You're different from anyone else I know. You're a good boy; when you are grown up you shall have a yoke of oxen, over and above your wages."

"This is very gratifying indeed," observed Pringle. "But—a sweetly solemn thought comes to me. You were going to tell me about another boy—the onliest little boy?"

"He's not a boy," said Stella, flushing hotly. "He's a man—a man's man. You'll like him, John Wesley—he's just your kind. I'm not going to tell you. You'll see him at our house, with the others. And he'll be the very one you'd pick out for me yourself. Of course you'll want to tease me by pretending to guess someone else; but you'll know which one he is, without me telling you. He stands out apart from all other men in every way. Come on, John Wesley—it's time to go down to the station."

Pringle caught step with her.

"And how long—if a reliable old faithful John may ask—before you become Stella Some-One-Else?"

"At Christmas. And I am a very lucky girl, John. What an absurd convention it is that people are never supposed to congratulate the girl—as if no man was ever worth having! Silly, isn't it?"

"Very silly. But then, it's a silly world."

"A delightful world," said Stella, her eyes sparkling. "You don't know how happy I am. Or perhaps you do know. Tell me honestly, did you ever l—like anyone, this way?"

"I refuse to answer, by advice of counsel," said John Wesley. "I'll say this much, though. X marks no spot where any Annie Laurie[11] gave me her promise true."

When the train had gone John Wesley wandered disconsolately back to his hotel and rested his elbows on the bar. The white-aproned attendant hastened to serve him.

"What will it be, sir?"

"Give me a gin pitfall," said John Wesley.

---

10 "Faithful John" or "Faithful Johannes," a German fairy tale published in English translation by the Brothers Grimm in 1819.

11 The Scottish song "Annie Laurie" celebrates a marriage proposal.

CHAPTER II

"COLD FEET?"

"Horrible!" said Anastacio.

Matthew Lisner, sheriff of Doña Ana, bent a hard eye on his subordinate.

"It's got to be done," he urged. "To elect our ticket we must have all the respectable and responsible people of the valley. If we can provoke Foy into an outbreak—"

"Not we—you," corrected Anastacio. "Myself, I do not feel provoking."

"Are you going to lay down on me?"

"If you care to put it that way—yes. Kit Foy is just the man to leave alone."

"Now, listen!" said the sheriff impatiently. "Half the valley is owned by newcomers, men of substance, who, with the votes they influence or control, will decide the election. Foy is half a hero with them, because of these vague old stories. But let him be stirred up to violence now and you'll see! They won't see any romance in it—just an open outrage; they will flock to us to the last man. Ours is the party of law and order—"

"Law *to* order, some say."

The veins swelled in the sheriff's heavy face and thick neck; he regarded his deputy darkly.

"That comes well from you, Barela![12] Don't you see, with the law on

12 Anastacio Barela (1872–1897), lawyer, politician, and deputy sheriff in Doña

our side all these men of substance will be with us unconditionally? I tell you, Christopher Foy is the brains of his party. Once he is discredited—"

"And I tell you that I am the brains of your party and I'll have nothing to do with your fine plan. 'Tis an old stratagem to call oppression, law, and resistance to oppression, lawlessness. You tried just that in ninety-six,[13] didn't you? And I never could hear that our side had any the best of it or that the good name of Doña Ana was in any way bettered by our wars. Come, Mr. Lisner—the Kingdom of Lady Ann has been quiet now for nearly eight years. Let us leave it so. For myself, the last row brought me reputation and place, made me chief deputy under two sheriffs—so I need have the less hesitation in setting forth my passionate preference for peace."

"You have as much to gain as I have," growled the sheriff. "Besides your own cinch, you have one of your *gente*[14] for deputy in every precinct in the county."

"Exactly! And if we have wars again, who but the Barelas would bear the brunt? No, no, Mr. Matt Lisner; while I may be a merely ornamental chief deputy, it will never be denied that I am a very careful chief to my *gente*. Be sure that I shall think more than once or twice before I set a man of my men at a useless hazard to pleasure you—or to reëlect you."

"You speak plainly."

"I intend to. I speak for three hundred—and we vote solid. Make no mistake, Mr. Lisner. You need me in your business, but I can do nicely without you."

"Perhaps you'd like to be sheriff yourself."

"I might like it—except that I am not as young and foolish as I was,"

Ana County in 1891 during the tenure of his uncle Mariano Barela as sheriff. See also "Fiction of Mexican Villain Exploded by Eugene M. Rhodes," *New York Tribune*, July 3, 1921, 53: "In a story of mine . . . I depicted a Mexican, Anastacio Barela, as a gallant rogue and loveable—such as he really was. . . . Anastacio and I were friends."

13 Barela refers obliquely to the disappearance and presumed murder for political reasons of Albert Jennings Fountain (b. 1838) and his young son near White Sands in 1896.

14 people

said Anastacio, smiling. "Now that I am so old, and so wise and all, it is clear to see that neither myself nor any of the fighting men of the mad old days—on either side—should be sheriff."

"You were not always so thoughtful of the best interests of the dear pee-pul," sneered the sheriff.

"That I wasn't. I was as silly and hot-brained a fool as either side could boast. But you, Sheriff, are neither silly nor hot-headed. In cold blood you are planning that men shall die; that other men shall rot in prison. Why? For hate and revenge? Not even that. Oh, a little spice of revenge, perhaps; Foy and his friends made you something of a laughing stock. But your main motive is—money. And I don't see why. You've got all the money any one man needs now."

"I notice you get your share."

"I hope so. But, even as a money-making proposition, your troubled-voters policy is a mistake. All the mountain men want is to be let alone, and you might be sheriff for life for all they care. But you fan up every little bicker into a lawsuit—don't I know? Just for the mileage—ten cents a mile each way in a county that's jam full of miles from one edge to the other; ten cents a mile each way for each and every arrest and subpoena. You drag them to court twice a year—the farmer at seed time and harvest, the cowman from the spring and fall round-ups. It hurts, it cripples them, they ride thirty miles to vote against you; it costs you all the extra mileage money to offset their votes. As a final folly, you purpose deliberately to stir up the old factions. What was it Napoleon said? 'It is worse than a crime: it is a blunder.'[15] I'll tell you now, not a Barela nor an Ascarate[16] shall stir a foot in such a quarrel. If you want to bait Kit Foy, do it yourself—or set your city police on him."

"I will."

A faint tinge of color came to the clear olive of Anastacio's cheek as he rose.

---

15 A quote attributed to Antoine Boulay de la Meurthe (1761–1840) about Napoleon's execution of Louis-Antoine-Henri de Bourbon-Condé, the Duc d'Enghien (b. 1772), in 1804.

16 Guadalupe Ascarte, a Democrat, was sheriff of Doña Ana County from 1894 until 1896.

"But don't promise my place to any of them, sheriff. I might hear of it."

"Stranger," said Ben Creagan, "you can't play pool! I can't—and I beat you four straight games. You better toddle your little trotters off to bed." The words alone might have been mere playfulness; glance and tone made plain the purposed offense.

The after-supper crowd in the hotel barroom had suddenly slipped away, leaving Max Barkeep, three others, and John Wesley Pringle—the last not unnoting of nudge and whisper attending the exodus. Since that, Pringle had suffered, unprotesting, more gratuitous insults than he had met in all the rest of his stormy years. His curiosity was aroused; he played the stupid, unseeing, patient, and timid person he was so eminently not. Plainly these people desired his absence; and Pringle highly resolved to know why. He now blinked mildly.

"But I'm not sleepy a-tall," he objected.

He tried and missed an easy shot; he chalked his cue with assiduous care.

"Here, you! Quit knockin' those balls round!" bawled Max, the bartender. "What you think this is—a kindergarten?"

"Why, I paid for all the games I lost, didn't I?" asked Pringle, much abashed.

He mopped his face. It was warm, though the windows and doors were open.

"Well, nobody's going to play any more with you," snapped Max. "You bore 'em."

He pyramided the balls and covered the table. With a sad and lingering backward look Pringle slouched abjectly through the wide-arched doorway to the bar.

"Come on, fellers—have something."

"Naw!" snarled José Espalin.[17] "I'm a-tryin' to theenk. Shut up, won't you?"

---

17 José Espalin, deputy sheriff of Doña Ana County (1898–1899) during Garrett's tenure as sheriff, was one of the posse charged with arresting Oliver Lee in 1898 for the Fountain murders.

Pringle sighed patiently at the rebuff and stole a timid glance at the thinker. Espalin was a lean little, dried-up manikin, with legs, arms, and mustaches disproportionately long for his dwarfish body. His black, wiry hair hung in ragged witchlocks; his black pin-point eyes were glittering, cold, and venomous. He looked, thought Pringle, very much like a spider.

"I'm steerin' you right, old man," said Creagan. "You'd better drag it for bed."

"I ain't sleepy, I tell you."

Espalin leaped up, snarling.

"Say! You lukeing for troubles, maybe? Bell, I theenk thees *hombre* got a gun. Shall we freesk him?"

As he flung the query over his shoulder his beady little eyes did not leave Pringle's.

Bell Applegate got leisurely to his feet—a tall man, well set up, with a smooth-shaved, florid face and red hair.

"If he has we'll jack him in the jug." He threw back the lapel of his coat, displaying a silver star.

"But I ain't got no gun," protested John Wesley meekly. "You-all can see for yourself."

"We will—don't worry! Don't you make one wrong move or I'll put out your light!"

"Be you the sheriff?"

"Police. Go to him, Ben!"

"No gun," reported Ben after a swift search of the shrinking captive.

"I done told you so, didn't I?"

"Mighty good thing for you, old rooster. Gun-toting is strictly barred in Las Uvas. You got to take your gun off fifteen minutes after you get in from the road and you can't put it on till fifteen minutes before you take the road again."

"Is that—er—police regulations or state law?"

"State law—and has been any time these twenty-five years. Say, you doddering old fool, what do you think this is—a night school?"

"I—I guess I'll go to bed," said Pringle miserably.

"I—I guess if you come back I'll throw you out," mimicked Ben with a guffaw.

Pringle made no answer. He shuffled into the hall and up the stairway to his bedroom. He unlocked the door noisily; he opened it noisily; he took his six-shooter and belt from the wall quietly and closed the door, noisily again; he locked it—from the outside. Then he did a curious thing; he sat down very gently and removed his boots.

The four in the barroom listened, grinning. When they heard Pringle's door slam shut Bell Applegate nodded and Creagan went out on the street. Behind him, at a table near the pool-room door, the law planned ways and means in a slinking undertone.

"You keep in the background, Joe. Let us do the talking. Foy just naturally despises you—we might not get him to stay the fifteen minutes out. You stay back there. Remember now, don't shoot till Ben lets him get his arm loose. *Sabe?*"

"Maybe Meester Ben don't find heem."

"Oh, yes, he will. Ditch meeting to-night. Ought to be out about now. Setting the time to use the water and assessing *fatiga*[18] work. Every last man with a water right will be there, sure, and Foy's got a dozen. Max, you are to be a witness, remember, and you mustn't be mixed up in it. Got your story straight?"

"Foy he comes in and makes a war-talk about Dick Marr," recited Max. "After we powwow awhile you see his gun. You tell him he's under arrest for carryin' concealed weapons. You and Ben grabbed his arm; he jerked loose and went after his gun. And then Joe shot him."

"That's it. We'll all stick to that. S-st! Here they come!"

There are men whose faces stand out in a crowd, men you turn to look after on the street. Such—quite apart from his sprightly past—was Christopher Foy, who now entered with Creagan. He was about thirty, above middle height, every mold and line of him slender and fine and strong. His face was resolute, vivacious, intelligent; his eyes were large and brown, pleasant and fearless. A wide black hat, pushed back now, showed a broad

---

18 fatiguing

forehead white against crisp coal-black hair and the pleasant tan of neck and cheek. But it was not his dark, forceful face alone that lent him such distinction. Rather it was the perfect poise and balance of the man, the ease and unconscious grace of every swift and sure motion. He wore a working garb now—blue overalls and a blue rowdy. But he wore them with an air that made him well dressed.

Foy paused for a second; Applegate rose.

"Well, Chris!" he laughed. "There has been a time when you might not have fancied this particular bunch—hey? All over now, please the pigs. Come in and give it a name. Beer for mine."

"I'll smoke," said Foy.

"Me too," said Espalin.

He lit a cigar and returned to his chair. Ben Creagan passed behind the bar and handed over a six-shooter and a cartridge belt.

"Here, Chris—here's the gun I borrowed of you when I broke mine. Much obliged."

Foy twirled the cylinder to make sure the hammer was on an empty chamber and buckled the belt under his rowdy.

"My hardware is mostly plows and scrappers and irrigating hoes nowadays," he remarked. "Good thing too."

"All the same, Foy, I'd keep a gun with me if I were you. Dick Marr is drinking again—and when he soaks it up he gets discontented over old times, you know." Applegate lowered his voice, with a significant glance at Espalin. "He threatened your life to-day. I thought you ought to know it."

Foy considered his cigar.

"That's awkward," he replied briefly.

"Chris," said Ben, "this isn't the first time. Dick's heart is bad to you. I'm sorry. He was my friend and you were not. But you're not looking for any trouble now. Dick is. And I'm afraid he'll keep on till he gets it. Me and the sheriff we managed to get him off to bed, but he says he's going to shoot you on sight—and I believe he means it. You ought to have him bound over to keep the peace."

Foy smiled and shook his head.

"I can't do that—and it would only make him madder than ever. But

I'll get out of his way and keep out of his way. I'll go up to the Jornado to-night and stay with the Bar Cross boys awhile. He won't come up there."

"You'll enjoy having people tellin' how you run away to keep from meeting Dick Marr?" said Applegate incredulously.

"Why shouldn't they say it? It will be exactly true," responded Foy quietly, "and you're authorized to say so. I'm learning some sense now; I'm getting to own quite a mess of property; I'm going to be married soon; and I don't want to fight anyone. Besides, quite apart from my own interests, other men will be drawn into it if I shoot it out with Marr. No knowing where it will stop. No, sir; I'll go punch cows till Marr quiets down. Maybe it's just the whisky talking. Dick isn't such a bad fellow when he's not fighting booze. Or maybe he'll go away. He hasn't much to keep him here."

"Say, I could get a job offered to him out in San Simon,"[19] said Applegate, brightening.

His eye rested on the clock over the long mirror. He stepped over to the show case, clipped the end from a cigar and obtained a light from a shapely bronze lady with a torch. When he came back he fell in on Foy's left; at Foy's right Creagan leaned his elbows on the bar.

"Well, I'm obliged to you, boys," said Foy. "This one's on me. Come on, Joe—have a hoot."

"Thanks, no," said Espalin. "I not dreenkin' none thees times. Eef I dreenk some I get full, and loose my job maybe."

"Vichy," said Foy. "Take something yourself, Max."

As Mr. Max poured the drinks an odd experience befell Mr. José Espalin. His tilted chair leaned against the casing of the billiard-room door. As Max filled the first glass Espalin became suddenly aware of something round and hard and cold pressed against his right temple. Mr. Espalin felt some curiosity, but he sat perfectly still. The object shifted a few inches; Mr. Espalin perceived from the tail of his eye the large, unfeeling muzzle of a six-shooter; beyond it, a glimpse of the forgotten elderly stranger, Mr. Pringle.

Only Mr. Pringle's fighting face appeared, and that but for a moment;

19 A village in eastern Arizona.

he laid a finger to lip and crouched, hidden by the partition and by Espalin's body. Mr. Espalin gathered that Pringle desired no outcry and shunned observation; he sat motionless accordingly; he felt a hand at his belt, which removed his gun.

"Happy days!" said Foy, and raised his glass to his lips.

Creagan seized the uplifted wrist with both hands, Applegate pounced on the other arm. Pringle leaped through the doorway. But something happened swifter than Pringle's swift rush. Foy's knee shot up to Applegate's stomach. Applegate fell, sprawling. Foy hurled himself on Creagan and bore him crashing to the floor. Foy whirled over; he rose on one hand and knee, gun drawn, visibly annoyed; also considerably astonished at the unexpected advent of Mr. Pringle. Applegate lay groaning on the floor. Pringle kicked his gun from the holster and set foot upon it; one of his own guns covered the bartender and the other kept watch on Espalin, silent on his still-tilted chair.

"Who're you!" challenged Foy.

"Friend with the countersign. Don't shoot! Don't shoot me, anyhow."

Foy rose from hand and knee to knee and foot. This rescuer, so opportunely arrived from nowhere, seemed to be an ally. But to avoid mistakes, Foy's gun followed Pringle's motions, at the same time willing and able to blow out Creagan's brains if advisable. He also acquired Creagan's gun quite subconsciously.

"Let me introduce myself, gentlemen," said Pringle. "I'm Jack-in-a-Pinch, Little Friend of the Under Dog—see Who's This? page two-thirteen. My German friend, come out from behind that bar—hands up—step lively! Spot yourself! My Mexican friend, join Mr. Max. Move, you poisonous little spider—jump! That's better! Gentlemen—be seated! Right there—smack, slapdab on the floor. Sit down and think. Say! I'm serious. Am I going to have to kill some few of you just because you don't know who I am? I'll count three! One! two!—That's it. Very good—hold that—register anticipation! I am a worldly man," said Pringle with emotion, "but this spectacle touches me—it does indeed!"

"I'll get square with you!" gurgled Applegate, as fiercely as his breathless condition would permit.

"George—may I call you George? I don't know your name. You may get square with me, George—but you'll never be square with anyone. You are a rhomboidinaltitudinous isosohedronal catawampus,[20] George!"

George raved unprintably. He made a motion to rise, but reconsidered it as he noted the tension of Pringle's trigger finger.

"Don't be an old fuss-budget, George," said Pringle reprovingly. "Because I forgot to tell you—I've got my gun now—and yours. You won't need to arrest me, though, for I'm hitting the trail in fifteen minutes. But if I wasn't going—and if you had your gun—you couldn't arrest one side of me. You couldn't arrest one of my old boots! Listen, George! You heard this Chris-gentleman give his reasons for wanting peace? Yes? Well, it's oh-so-different here. I hate peace! I loathe, detest, abhor, and abominate peace! My very soul with strong disgust is stirred—by peace! I'm growing younger every year, I don't own any property here, I'm not going to be married; I ain't feeling pretty well anyhow; and if you don't think I'll shoot, try to get up! Just look as if you thought you wanted to wish to try to make an effort to get up."

"How—who—" began Creagan; but Pringle cut him short.

"Ask me no more, sweet! You have no speaking part here. We'll do the talking. I just love to talk. I am the original tongue-tied man; I ebb and flow. Don't let me hear a word from any of you! Well, pardner?"

Foy, still kneeling in fascinated amaze, now rose. Creagan's nose was bleeding profusely.

"That was one awful wallop you handed our gimlet-eyed friend," said Pringle admiringly. "Neatest bit of work I ever saw. Sir, to you! My compliments!" He placed a chair near the front door and sat down. "I feel like a lion in a den of Daniels,"[21] he sighed.

"But how did you happen to be here so handy?" inquired Foy.

"Didn't happen—I did it on purpose," said John Wesley. "You see, these four birds tipped their hand. All evening they been instructing me where I

20 A nonsense phrase.

21 Pringle invokes a cliched pun on Daniel 6:16: "they brought Daniel and cast him into the den of lions."

got off. They would-ed I had the wings of a dove, so I might fly far, far away and be at rest. Now, I put it to you, do I look like a dove?"

"Not at present," laughed Foy.

"Well, I didn't like it—nobody would. I see there was a hen on, I knew the lay of the ground from looking after my horse. So I clomped off to bed, got my good old Excalibur gun—full name X.L.V. Caliber[22]—slipped off my boots, tippytoed down the back stairs like a Barred Rock cat, oozed in by the side door—and here I be! I overheard their pleasant little plan to do you. I meant to do the big rescue act, but you mobilize too quick for me. All the same, maybe it's as well I chipped in, because—take a look at them cartridges in your gun, will you? Your own gun—the one they borrowed from you."

Foy twisted a bullet from a cartridge. There was no powder. The four men on the floor looked unhappy under his thoughtful eye.

"Nice little plant—what? Do we kill 'em?" said Pringle cheerfully. "I don't know the rules well enough to break them. What was the big idea? Was they vexed at you, son?"

"It would seem so," said Foy, smiling. "We had a little war here a spell back. I suspect they wanted to stir it up again for political effect. Election this fall."

"And you were not in their party? I see!" said Pringle, nodding intelligently, "Well, they sure had it fixed to make your side lose one vote—fixed good and proper. The Ben-boy was to let your right hand loose and the Joe-boy was to shoot you as you pulled your gun. Why, if you had lived to make a statement your own story woulda mighty near let them out."

"I believe that I am greatly obliged to you, sir."

"I believe you are," said Pringle. "And—but, also, I know the two gentlemen you were drinking with should be very grateful to you. They had just half a second more to live—and you beat me to it. Too bad! Well, what next?"

---

22 A double-barrel .45 revolver. McEwen puns on "Excalibur," the charmed sword of King Arthur that figures prominently in Thomas Malory's *Morte d'Arthur* (1485) and Tennyson's *Idylls of the King* (1859–1885).

Foy pondered a little.

"I guess I'll go up to the Bar Cross wagon, as I intended, till things simmer down. The Las Uvas warriors seldom ever bother the Bar Cross Range. My horse is hitched up the street. How'd you like to go along with me, stranger? You and me would make a fair-sized crowd."

"I'd like it fine and dandy," said Pringle. "But I got a little visit to make to-morrow. Maybe I'll join you later. I like Las Uvas," stated John Wesley, beaming. "Nice, lively little place! I think I'll settle down here after a bit. Some of the young fellows are shy on good manners. But I can teach 'em. I'd enjoy it. . . . Now, let's see: If you'll hold these lads a few minutes I'll get my boots and saddle up and bring my horse to the door; then I'll pay Max my hotel bill and talk to them while you get your horse; and we'll ride together till we get out in the open. How's that for a lay?"

That was a good lay, it seemed; and it was carried out—with one addition: After Foy brought his horse he rang Central[23] and called up the sheriff.

"Hello! That you, Mr. Lisner? This is Kitty Foy," he said sweetly. "Sheriff, I hate to bother you, but old Nueces River, your chief of police, is out of town. And I thought you ought to know that the police force is all balled up. They're here at the Gadsden Purchase. Bell Applegate is sick—seems to be indigestion; Espalin is having a nervous spell; and Ben Creagan is bleeding from his happiest vein. You'd better come see to 'em. Good-bye!"

Pringle smiled benevolently from the door.

"There! I almost forgot to tell you boys. We disapprove of your actions oh-very-much! You know you were doing what was very, very wrong—like three little mice that were playing in the barn though the old mouse said: 'Little mice, beware! When the owl comes singing "Too-whoo" take care!'[24] If you do it again we shall consider it deliberately unfriendly of you. . . . Well, I'll toddle my decrepit old bones out of this. Eleven o'clock!

23 Called the local telephone operator.

24 "The Owls and the Mice," a popular nineteenth-century children's song. A version is printed in its entirety in the *Santa Cruz Sentinel*, April 19, 1908, 6.

How time has flown, to be sure! Thank you for a pleasant evening. Good-by, George. Good-by, all! Be good little boys—go nighty-nighty!"

They raced to the corner, scurried down the first side street, turned again, and slowed to a gallop. Pringle was in high feather; he caroled blithesome as he rode:

So those three little owls flew back up in the barn—
Inky, dinky, doodum, day!

And they said, "Those little mice make us feel so nice and warm!"
Inky, dinky, doodum, day!

Then they all began to sing, "Too-whit! Too-who!"
I don't think much of this song, do you?

But there's one thing about it—'tis certainly true—
Inky, dinky, doodum, day!

They reached the open; the gallop became a trot.

"I go north here," said Foy at the cross-roads above the town. "Which way for you?"

"North too," said Pringle. "I don't know just where, but you can tell me. I go to a railroad station first—Aden. Then to the Vorhis place."

"Vorhis? I'm going there myself?" said Foy. "You didn't tell me your name yet."

"Pringle."

"What? Not John Wesley Pringle? Great Scott, man! I've heard Stella talk about you a thousand times. Say, I'm sure glad to meet you! My name's Foy—Christopher Foy."

"Why, yes," said Pringle. "I think I've heard Stella speak of you, too."

CHAPTER III

BEING A CHILD MUST have been great fun—once. Nowadays one would as lief be a Strasbourg goose.[25] When you and I went to school it was not quite so bad. True, neither of us could now extract a cube root with a stump puller, and it is sad to reflect how little call life has made for duodecimals. Sometimes it seems that all our struggle with moody verbs and insubordinate conjunctions was a wicked waste—poor little sleepy puzzleheads! But there were certain joyous facts which we remember yet. Lake Erie was very like a whale; Lake Ontario was a seal; and Italy was a boot.

The great Chihuahuan desert is a boot too; a larger boot than Italy. The leg of it is in Mexico, the toe is in Arizona, the heel in New Mexico; and the Jornado is in the boot-heel.

El Jornado del Muerto—the Journey of the Dead Man! From what dim old legend has the name come down? No one knows. The name has outlived the story.

Perhaps some grim, hard-riding Spaniard made his last ride here; weary at last of war, turned his dead face back to Spain and the pleasant valleys of his childhood. We have a glimpse of him, small in the mighty silence; his faithful few about him, with fearful backward glances; a gray sea of waving grama breaking at their feet; the great mountains looking down on them. Plymouth Rock is unnamed yet.—Then the mist shuts down.

The Santa Fé Trail reaches across the Jornado; tradition tells of vague,

25 Geese fattened for pâté de foie gras.

wild battles with Apache and Navajo; there are grave-cairns on lone dim ridges, whereon each passer casts a stone. Young mothers dreamed over the cradles of those who now sleep here, undreaming; here is the end of all dreams.

Doniphan[26] passed this way; Kit Carson[27] rode here; the Texans journeyed north along that old road in '62[28]—to return no more.

These were but passers-by. The history of the Jornado, of indwellers named and known, begins with six Americans, as follows: Sandoval, a Mexican; Toussaint, a Frenchman; Fest, a German; Martin, a German; Roullier, a Swiss; and Teagardner, a Welshman.[29]

You might have thought the Jornado a vast and savage waste or a pleasant place and a various. That depended upon you. Materials for either opinion were plenty; lava flow, saccaton flats, rolling sand hills sage-brush, mesquite and yucca, bunch grass and shallow lakes, bench and hill, ridge and groundswell and wandering draw; always the great mountains round about; the mountains and the warm sun overall.

---

26 Alexander W. Doniphan (1808–1887), colonel of a Missouri regiment that was deployed in New Mexico during and after the Mexican-American War.

27 Kit Carson (1809–1868), frontier guide and trapper.

28 In late March 1862, during the only significant battle of the Civil War in New Mexico, a Confederate brigade from Texas under the command of Henry Hopkins Sibley (1816–1886) was repulsed at Glorieta Pass a few miles from Santa Fe.

29 Rhodes mentions several citizens in Sierra County, New Mexico, with whom he was acquainted as a young man: Pedro José Sandoval (d. 1893), a rancher near Hillsboro, New Mexico; Henry or Henry G. Toussant (d. 1896), a ranger near Engle; Edward Fest (d. 1892), a merchant in Cuchillo Negro, New Mexico, and local Democratic politician; Bob Martin (1873–1965), of Hot Springs and Hillsboro, punched cattle with Rhodes at the Bar Cross ranch in the 1890s; August E. Roullier (d. 1914), a merchant and rancher in Sierra and Valencia counties; and Ben Teagardner, a well-known Sierra County ranch hand. Rhodes featured his friend Teagardner by name in several stories, including "The Fool's Heart," *Saturday Evening Post*, May 1, 1915 ("He was a very old man—tough and sturdy and straight and tall for all that" and "he had come back to the land of his youth—to die") and "No Mean City," *Saturday Evening Post*, May 17–24, 1919 ("the oldest of old timers"). Rhodes left an incomplete novel about Teagardner titled "Road to Nowhere" when he died (Hutchinson, *A Bar Cross Man*, 169n33).

A certain rich man desired to be President—to please his wife, perhaps. He was a favorite son sure of his home-state vote in any grand old national convention. He gave largely to charities and campaign funds, and his left hand would have been justly astonished to know what his right hand was about.

Those were bargain-counter days. Fumbling the wares, our candidate saw, among other things, that New Mexico had six conventional votes: He sent after them.

So the Bar Cross Cattle Company was founded; range, the Jornado. Our candidate provided the money and a manager, also ambidextrous with instructions to get those votes and incidentally to double the money, as a good and faithful manager should.

He got the six votes, but our candidate never became president. Poor fellow, his millions could not bring him happiness. He died, an embittered and disappointed man, in the obscurity of the United States Senate.[30]

The Bar Cross brand was the sole fruit of that ambition. Other ranches had dwindled or vanished; favored by environment the Bar Cross, almost alone, withstood the devastating march of progress. It was still a mark of distinction to be a Bar Cross man. The good old customs—and certain bad old customs, too—still held on the Bar Cross Range, fifty miles by one hundred, on the Jornado. Scattered here and there were smaller ranches: among them the V H—the Vorhis Ranch.

Stella Vorhis and John Wesley, far out on the plain, rode through the pleasant afternoon. The V H Ranch was in sight now, huddled low before

---

30 Russell A. Alger (1836–1907), a Civil War general, businessman, former governor of Michigan, Republican candidate for president in 1888, secretary of war under William McKinley, and US senator. According to John W. Leonard (*Industries of Detroit* [Detroit: Elstner, 1887], 248), Alger invested heavily in lumber companies, banks, and "a cattle ranch in New Mexico," apparently the Bar Cross, which was nicknamed "the Detroit Ranch" (C. L. Sonnichsen, *Tularosa: Last of the Frontier West* [New York: Devin-Adair, 1960], 170). See also *Santa Fe New Mexican*, April 14, 1888, 2: Alger was "largely interested in New Mexico and the territory's interest would be well looked after in the event of his nomination and election."

them; beyond, a cluster of low hills rose from the plain, visible center of a world fresh, eager, and boundless.

The girl's eye kindled with delight as it sought the far horizons, the misty parapets gleaming up through the golden air; she was one who found dear and beautiful this gray land, silent and ensunned. She flung up her hand exultingly.

"Isn't it wonderful, John Wesley? Do you know what it makes me think of? This:

Magic casements, opening on the foam
Of perilous seas, in faëry lands forlorn![31]

"Think, John! This country hasn't changed a bit since the day Columbus set out from Spain."

"How true! Fine old bird, Columbus—he saw America first. Great head he showed, too, getting himself named Christopher. Otherwise you might have said, 'the day Antony discovered Cleopatra'[32]—or something like that. Wise old Chris!"

Stella's eyes narrowed reflectively.

"John Wesley, you've been reading! You never used to know anything about Mark Antony."

"I cribbed that remark from Billy Beebe and he swiped it from a magazine. I don't know much about Mark, even this very yet. Good old easy Mark!"

"That's the how of it. You've been absorbing knowledge from those pardners of yours. Your talk shows it. You're changed a lot—that way. Every other way you're the same old Wes!"

"Now, that sounds better!" said Pringle in his most complacent tones.

"I want to talk about myself, always, Stella May Vorhis; we've come thirty miles and I've heard Christopher Foy, Foy, Foy, all the way! It's exasperating! It's sickening!"

---

31 The final lines of stanza 7 in "Ode to a Nightingale" (1819) by the English poet John Keats (1795–1821).

32 Shakespeare's tragedy *Antony and Cleopatra* (ca. 1607).

But Stella was not to be flustered. She held her head proudly.

"It's you that have been talking about him. I told you you'd like him, John Wesley."

"Yes, you did—and I do. He's a self-starter. He's a peppermist. He's a regular guy. It wasn't only the way he smashed those thugs—taken by surprise and all—but that he had judgment enough not to shoot when there was no need for it; that's what gets me! And then he went and spoiled it all."

"How?"

"Hiking on up to the ranch with the Major, without even waking you up. Why, if it was me, do you s'pose I'd leave another man—no matter how old and safe he was—to tell such a story as that his own way and hog all the credit for himself? That Las Uvas push is a four-flush—he needn't stir a peg for them. No, sir! I'd have stayed right there till you got ready to come—and every time I'd narrate that tale about the scrap it would get scarier and scarier."

"I know, without telling, what my Chris does is the brave thing, the best thing," said the girl, with softly shining eyes. "And he never brags—any more than you do, Wes. You're always making fun of yourself. And I'm afraid you don't know how serious a menace this Las Uvas gang is. It isn't what Chris may do or may not do. All they want is a pretext. Why, John, there are men down there who are really quite truthful—as men go—till they get on the witness stand. But the minute they're under oath they begin to lie. Force of habit, I guess. The whole courthouse ring hates Chris and fears him—especially Matt Lisner, the sheriff. In the old trouble, whenever he was outwitted or outfought, Chris did it. Besides—" She paused; the color swept to her cheek.

"Besides—you. Yes, yes," grumbled Pringle. "Might have been expected. These women! Does the Foy-boy know?"

"He knows that Lisner wanted to marry me," said Stella. Neck and cheek were crimson now; but it was characteristic that her level eyes met Pringle's fearlessly. "But before that—he—he persecuted me, John. Chris must not know. He would kill him. But I wanted you to know in case anything happened to Chris. There is nothing they will stick at, these men.

Lisner is the vilest; he hates Chris worst of all." She was in deep distress; there were tears in her eyes as she smiled at him. "And I wish—oh, John Wesley, you don't know how I wish you were staying here—dear old friend!"

"As a dear and highly valuable old friend," said Pringle sedately, "let me point out how shrewd and sensible a plan it would be for you and your Chris to go on a honeymoon at once—and never come back."

"I am beginning to think so. Up to last night I had only my fears to go on."

"But now you know. We managed to make a joke of last night—but what that push had in mind was plain murder. I would dearly like," said John Wesley, "to visit Las Uvas—some dark night—in a Zeppelin."[33]

At the corral gate the Major met them, with a face so troubled that Stella cried out in alarm:

"Father! What is it? Chris?"

"Stella—be brave! Dick Marr was killed at midnight—and they're swearing it off on Chris."

"But John Wesley was with him."

"That's just it. Applegate and Creagan tell it that they saw Chris leaving town at eleven o'clock, that he said he was coming up here, and that he made a war-talk about Marr. But not a word about Pringle or the fight at the hotel. Joe Espalin doesn't appear—no claim that he saw Foy at all."

"That looks ugly," observed Pringle.

"Ugly! Your testimony is to be thrown out as a lie made of whole cloth. Espalin and the barkeeper don't appear. They're afraid the Mexican will get tangled up, and Max will swear he didn't see Chris at all. It's cut and dried. You are to be canceled. Marr was found this morning at the first crossroad above town. His watch was stopped at ten minutes to twelve—mashed, it seemed, where it hit on a stone when he fell. If they had told about the mix-up with you and Chris last night, I might have thought they really believed Chris killed Marr—or suspected it. As it stands, we know the whole thing is a black, rotten conspiracy."

33 A type of rigid aircraft named for its inventor and manufactured in Germany.

"But where's Chris?" demanded Stella, trembling.

"We have none of us seen Chris—you want to remember that. You won't have to lie, Stella—you didn't see him. Pringle, I bank on you."

"Sure! I can lie and stick to it, though I'm sadly out of practice," said Pringle. "But hadn't we better fix up the same history to tell? And where's your man Hargis[34] that stays here? Will he do?"

"Unsaddle and I'll tell you. We've only got a few minutes. I saw the dust of them coming down from the north as I drove in this bunch of saddle horses. Some of them went up by train to Upham, you know. Hargis has gone to the round-up, and I'm just as well pleased. I'm not sure he can be trusted. We are to know not the first word of what has happened. We haven't seen Chris and haven't heard of the murder. Come in—we'll start dinner and be taken by surprise. Pringle, throw your gun over on the bunk. Stella, get that look off your face. After you hear the news you can look any old way and it'll be natural enough. But you've got to be unconcerned and unsuspicious when they first come."

He started a fire. Stella set about preparing dinner.

"Who brought the news?" she asked.

"Joe Cowan[35]—and a relay. Someone rode to Jeff Isaacks's ranch[36] as fast as ever a horse could go. Jeff came to Quartzite; Dodd passed the word on to Goldenburg's[37] and Cowan came here. At every ranch they drove all the fresh saddle horses out of the way, so a posse couldn't get a remount without losing time. Kitty Foy has got good friends, and they don't believe he'd shoot any man in the back."

"And Foy's drifted with Cowan?"

"He hadn't a chance to get clear," said the Major. "We had no fresh horses here. They've sworn in a small army of deputies. Nearly a hundred

---

34 Rhodes reportedly feuded with Kentucky Hargis, a southern New Mexico wrangler (Marc Simmons, "Why Gene Rhodes Fled New Mexico," *Santa Fe Reporter*, January 16, 1991, 10). See also Frank M. Clark, 34.

35 Rhodes also referred in *Good Men and True* (New York: Holt, 1914), 141, to "red-headed Joe Cowan, cowboy, of Organ," New Mexico.

36 Jeff Isaacks (d. 1928), rancher in Doña Ana County, New Mexico.

37 Max B. Goldenburg (1857–1940), another rancher in Doña Ana County.

men are out hunting for him by this time. One posse was to go up the San Andrés on the east, leaving a man at every waterhole. The sheriff wired for a special train, took a carload of saddle horses and dropped a couple of men off at every station. At Upham the rest of them were to unload and string out across the Jornado, so as to cut Chris off from the Bar Cross round-up at Aleman. It's some of that bunch I saw coming, I guess. And the others were to scatter out and come up the middle of the plain. They'll drag the Jornado with a fine-toothed comb."

"How's he to get away, then?"

"Cowan took Kit's horse and led his own, which was about give out. He turned back east, up a draw where he won't be seen unless somebody's right on top of him. Eight or ten miles out he'll turn Foy's horse loose; he'll carry the extra saddle on a ways and drop it in a washout. They'll find Foy's horse and think he's roped a fresh one. Then Cowan will start up a fresh bunch of mares and raise big dust. He will ride straight to the first posse he sees, claiming he's run his horse down chasing the mares. That'll let him out—maybe."

"And Foy?"

"We rode my horse double to the edge of the hills, to where he could walk on a ledge and leave no tracks," said the Major. "Then I went on. I rounded up this bunch of saddle horses and brought them back. He went up on Little Thumb Butte. It's all bluffs and bowlders there.[38] Up on the highest big cliff, at the very top, is a deep crack that winds up in a cave like a tunnel. You know the place, Stella?"

"Yes. But, dad, they'll hunt out the hills the first thing."

"They will not!" said the Major triumphantly. "They'll read our sign; they'll see where four shod horses came up the road. I'll claim one of them was a horse I was leading—that'll be that bald-faced roan out in the corral. We all want to stick to that."

"But he's bigger than any of our horses," objected Pringle. "They'll know better by the tracks."

38 Rhodes noted in "A Touch of Nature," *Out West* 29 (July 1908), 76, that Thumb Butte, located in Prescott National Forest, Arizona, was "cliff-walled on three sides" and commanded a view of "the whole Tip-Top country."

"Exactly! So they'll find a fresh-shod track going east—a track matching the fourth track we left on the road. They'll reason that we're trying to keep them from following that track. So they'll follow it up; they'll find Kit's give-out horse and then they'll know they're right."

"It seems to me," said Pringle reflectively, "that friend Cowan may have an interesting time if they get him."

The Major permitted himself a grin.

"He yanked the shoes off his horse before he left. Once he mixes his tracks up with a bunch of wild mares he'll be all right. They may think, but they can't prove anything. And Foy'll be all right—if only the posse follows the plain trail."

"It's too much to hope," said Stella. "They'll split up. Some of them will hunt out the hills anyway—to-morrow, if not to-day."

"That's my idea of it," said Pringle.

"They won't find the cave if they do," said Vorhis hopefully. "If he can get to the Bar Cross they'll see him through, once they hear his story. Not telling about that clean-up you and Kit made last night is a dead give-away."

"Any chance of Foy slipping out afoot?"

"Too far. But he could stand a siege till we could get word to his friends if, by any chance, the posse should find his cave. He took my rifle. He can see them coming; he'll have every advantage against attack; and there's another way out of the cave, up on top of the hill. There's just one thing against him. There wasn't even a canteen here. He took some jerky and canned stuff—but only one measly beer bottle of water. When that's used up it's going to be a dull time for him. We can't get water to him very handy without leaving some sign. We mustn't get hostile with the posse. Take it easy—you especially, Pringle. Stella and me, they know where we stand. But you're a stranger. Maybe they'll let you go on. If you once get away—bring the Bar Cross boys and they'll take Foy out of here in broad day."

"Very pretty—but there's four men in Las Uvas that know me—and three of them are police. Maybe they'll stay in the city though—being police?"

"No, they won't," said the Major gloomily. "They'll be along—deputized, of course. Maybe they won't be in the first batch though. Your part is to be the disinterested traveler, wanting to be on your way."

"It won't work, Major. This is a put-up job. Even if Applegate and his strikers aren't along they've given my description. Somebody will know I was with Foy last night, and they'll know I'm lying."

The Major sighed. "That's so, too. I'm afraid you're in for trouble."

"I'm used to that," said Pringle lightly. "Once, in Arizona—"

"Don't throw it up to me, John," said the Major a trifle sheepishly. "I'll say this though: I wouldn't ask for a better man in a tight than you."

"Thanks so much!" murmured Pringle. "And that Sir Hubert Stanley thing."[39]

"One more point, John: You don't know Foy. I do. Foy'll never give up. He's desperate—and he's not pleased. There's no question of surrender and standing trial; understand that. He'd be lynched, probably, if they ever got him in Las Uvas. A trial, even, would be just lynching under another name. They don't want to capture him anyway—they want a chance to kill him."

"I wouldn't want the job," said Pringle.

"Hush!" said Stella. "I hear them coming. Talk about something else—the war in Europe."

The Major picked up a paper.

"What do you think about the United States building a big navy, John?" he asked casually.

Stealthy footsteps rustled without.

"Fine!" said Pringle. "I'm strong for it. We want dreadnoughts, and lots of 'em—biggest we can build. But that ain't all. When we make the navy appropriations we ought to set by about fifty-some-odd million and build a big multiple-track railroad, so we can carry our navy inland in case of war. The ocean is no place for a battleship these days."

---

39 Sir Hubert Stanley, a debt-ridden aristocrat who persuades his son to marry his creditor's daughter in the five-act comedy *A Cure for the Heart-ache* (1797) by Thomas Morton (1764–1838).

"Stop your kidding!"

"I'm not kidding," said John Wesley indignantly. "I never was twice as serious in my whole life. My plan is sound, statesmanlike—"

"Shut up, you idiot! I want to read."

"Oh, very well, then! I'll grind the coffee."

Men crept close to the open door on each side of the kitchen. Stella slipped a pan of biscuits in the oven; she laid the table briskly, with a merry clatter of tinware; her face was cheerful and unclouded. The Major leaned back in one chair, his feet on another; he was deep in the paper; he puffed his pipe. John Wesley Pringle twirled the coffee mill between his knees and sang a merry tune:

There were three little mice, playing in the barn—
Inky, dinky, doodum, day!
Though they knew they were doing what was very, very wrong—
Inky, dinky, doodum, day!
And the song of the owls, it sounded so nice
That closer and closer crept the three little mice.
And the owls came and gobbled them—

A shadow fell across the floor.

"Hands up!" said the sheriff of Doña Ana. "We want Chris Foy!"

CHAPTER IV

NAVAJO, PIMA, AND HOPI enjoy seven cardinal points—north, east, west, south, up, down, and right here. In these and any intermediate directions from the Vorhis Ranch the diligent posse comitatus made swift and jealous search through the slow hours of afternoon. It commandeered the V H Saddle horses in the corral; it searched for sign in the soft earth of the wandering draws between the dozen low hills scattered round Big Thumb Butte and Little Thumb Butte; it rode circles round the ranch; the sign of Christopher Foy's shod horse was found and followed hotfoot by a detachment. Eight men had arrived in the first bunch, with the sheriff; others from every angle joined by twos and threes from hour to hour till the number rose to above a score. A hasty election provided a protesting cook and a horse wrangler; a V H beef was slaughtered.

The posse was rather equally divided between two classes—simpletons and fools. The first unquestionably believed Foy to be a base and cowardly murderer, out of law, whom it were most righteous to harry; else, as the storied juryman put it, "How came he there?" The other party were of those who hold that evildoing may permanently prosper and endure.

In the big living room of the adobe ranch house much time had been wasted in cross-questions and foolish answers. Stella Vorhis had been banished to her own room and Sheriff Matt Lisner had privately told off a man to make sure she did not escape.

Lisner and Ben Creagan, crossest of the four examiners, had been prepared to meet by crushing denial an eager and indignant statement from

Pringle, adducing the Gadsden House affair and his subsequent companying with Foy as proof positive of Foy's innocence. That no such accusation came from Pringle set these able but mystified deniers entirely at a loss, left the denial high and dry. Creagan mopped his brow furtively.

"Vorhis," said Sheriff Matt, red and angry from an hour's endeavor, "I think you're telling a pack of lies—every word of it. You know mighty well where Foy is."

"Guess I'll tell you lies if I want to," he retorted defiantly.

"But, Sheriff, he may be telling us the truth," urged Paul Breslin. "Foy may very well have ridden here alone before Vorhis got here. I've known the Major a long time. He isn't the man to protect a red-handed murderer."

"Aw, bah! How do you know I won't? How do you know he's a murderer? You make me sick!" declared the Major hotly. Breslin was an honest, well-meaning farmer; the Major was furious to find such a man allied with Foy's foes—certain sign that other decent blockheads would do likewise. "Matt Lisner tells you Kit Foy is a murderer and you believe him implicitly: Matt Lisner tells you I'm a liar—but you stumble at that. Why? Because you think about me—that's why! Why don't you try that plan about Foy—thinking?"

"But Foy's run away," stammered Breslin, disconcerted.

"Run away, hell! He's not here, you mean. According to your precious story, Foy was leaving before Marr was killed—or before you say Marr was killed. Why don't you look for him with the Bar Cross round-up? There's where he started for, you say?"

"I wired up and had a trusty man go out there quietly at once. He's staying there still—quietly," said the sheriff. "Foy isn't there—and the Bar Cross hasn't heard of the killing yet. It won't do, Major. Foy's run away."

John Wesley Pringle, limp, slack, and rumpled in his chair, yawned, stretching his arms wide.

"This man Foy," he ventured amiably, "if he really run away, he done a wise little stunt for himself, I think. Because every little ever and anon, thin scraps of talk float in from your cookfire in the yard—and there's a heap of it about ropes and lynching, for instance. If he hasn't run away yet, he'd better—and I'll tell him so if I see him. Stubby, red-faced, spindlin', thickset, jolly little man, ain't he? Heavy-complected, broad-shouldered, dark blond, very tall and slender, weighs about a hundred and ninety, with a pale skin and a hollow-cheeked, plump, serious face?"

At this ill-timed and unthinkable levity Breslin stared in bewilderment; Lisner glared, gripping his fist convulsively; and Mr. Ben Creagan, an uneasy third inquisitor, breathed hard through his nose; the fourth and last inquisitor, maintained unmoved the disinterested attitude he had held since the interrogation began. Feet crossed, he lounged in his chair, graceful, silent, smoking, listening, idly observant of wall and ceiling.

No answer being forthcoming to his query Pringle launched another:

"Speaking of faces, Creagan, old sport, what's happened to you and your nose? You look like someone had spread you on the minutes." He eyed Creagan with solicitous interest.

Mr. Creagan's battered face betrayed emotion. Pringle's shameless mendacity shocked him. But it was Creagan's sorry plight that he must affect never to have seen this insolent Pringle before. The sheriff's face mottled with wrath. Pringle reflected swiftly: The sheriff's rage hinted strongly that he was in Creagan's confidence and hence was no stranger to last night's mishap at the hotel; their silence proclaimed their treacherous intent.

On the other hand, these two, if not the others, knew very well that Pringle had left town with Foy and had probably stayed with him; that the Major must know all that Foy and Pringle knew. Evidently, Pringle decided, these two, at least, could expect no direct information from their persistent questionings; what they hoped for was unconscious betrayal by some slip of the tongue. As for young Breslin, Pringle had long since sized him up for what the Major knew him to be—a good-hearted, right-meaning simpleton. In the indifferent-seeming Anastacio, Pringle recognized an unknown quantity.

That, for a certainty, Christopher Foy had not killed Marr, was a positive bit of knowledge which Pringle shared only with the murderer himself and with that murderer's accomplices, if any. So much was plain, and Pringle felt a curiosity, perhaps pardonable, as to who the murderer really was.

Duty and inclination thus happily wedded, Pringle set himself to goad ferret-eyed Creagan and the heavy-jawed sheriff into unwise speech. And inattentive Anastacio had a shrewd surmise at Pringle's design. He knew nothing of the fight at the Gadsden House, but he sensed an unexplained tension—and he knew his chief.

"And this man, too—what about him?" said Breslin, regarding Pringle with a puzzled face. "Granted that the Major might have a motive for shielding Foy—he may even believe Foy to be innocent—why should this stranger put himself in danger for Foy?"

"Here, now—none of that!" said Pringle with some asperity. "I may be a stranger to you, but I'm an old friend of the Major's. I'm his guest, eating his grub and drinking his baccy; if he sees fit to tell any lies I back him up, of course. Haven't you got any principle at all? What do you think I am?"

"I know what you are," said the sheriff. "You're a damned liar!"

"An amateur only," said Pringle modestly. "I never take money for it." He put by a wisp of his frosted hair, the better to scrutinize, with insulting slowness, the sheriff's savage face. "Your ears are very large!" he murmured at last. "And red!"

The sheriff leaped up.

"You insolent cur-dog!" he roared.

"'To stand and be still to the Birken'ead drill is a dam' tough bullet to chew,'"[40] quoted Pringle evenly. "But he done it—old Pringle—John Wesley Pringle—liar and cur-dog too! We'll discuss the cur-dog later. Now, about the liar. You're mighty certain, seems to me. Why? How do you know I'm lying? For I am lying—I'll not deceive you. I'm lying; you know I'm lying; I know that you know I'm lying: and you apprehend clearly that I am aware that you are cognizant of the fact that I am fully assured that you know I am lying. Just like that! What a very peculiar set of happenstances! I am a nervous woman and this makes my head go round!"

"The worst day's work you ever did for yourself," said the angry sheriff, "was when you butted into this business."

---

40 In "Soldier an' Sailor Too" (1896), Kipling celebrated the "drill," originating with the sinking of the HMS *Birkenhead* off the coast of South Africa in 1852, that prioritized the safety of women and children.

"Yes, yes; go on. Was this to-day or yesterday—at the hotel?"

"Liar!" roared Lisner. "You never were at the Gadsden House."

"Who said I was?"

The words cracked like a whiplash. Simultaneously Pringle's tilted chair came down to its four legs and Pringle sat poised, his weight on the balls of his feet, ready for a spring. The sheriff paused midway of a step; his mottled face grew ashen. A gurgle very like a smothered chuckle came from Anastacio. Creagan flung himself into the breach.

"Aw, Matt, let's have the girl in here. We can't get nothing from these stiff-necked idiots."

"Might as well," agreed Lisner in a tone that tried to be contemptuous but trembled. "We're wasting time here."

"Lisner," said the Major in his gentlest tone, "be well advised and leave my daughter be."

"And if I don't?" sneered Lisner. He had no real desire to question Stella, but welcomed the change of venue as a diversion from his late indiscretion. "If, in the performance of my duty, I put a few civil questions to Miss Vorhis—in the presence of her father, mind you—then what?"

"But you won't!" said the Major softly.

"Do you know, Sheriff, I think the Major has the right idea?" said Pringle. "We won't bother the young lady."

"Who's going to stop me?"

Anastacio, in his turn, brought his chair to the floor, at the same time unclasping his hands from behind his head.

"I'll do that little thing, Sheriff," he announced mildly. "Miss Vorhis has already told us that she has not seen Foy since yesterday noon. That is quite sufficient."

Silence.

"This makes me fidgety. Somebody say something, quick—anything!" begged Pringle. "All right, then; I will. Let's go back—we've dropped a stitch. That goes about me being a liar and a damned one, Sheriff; but I'm hurt to have you think I'm a cur-dog. You're the sheriff, doin' your duty, as you so aptly observed. And you've done took my gun away. But if bein' a cur-dog should happen to vex me—honest, Sheriff, I'm that sensitive that

I'll tell you now—not hissing or gritting or gnashing my teeth—just telling you—the first time I meet you in a strictly private and unofficial way I'm goin' to remold you closer to my heart's desire!"

"You brazen hussy! You know you lied!"

"You're still harpin' on that, Sheriff? That doesn't make it any easier to be a cur-dog. How did you know I lied? You say so, mighty positive—but what are your reasons? Why don't you tell your associates? There is an honest man in this room. I am not sure there are not two—"

Anastacio's eyes again removed themselves from the ceiling.

"If you mean me—and somehow I am quite clear as to that—"

"I mean Mr. Breslin."

"Oh, him—of course!" said Anastacio in a shocked voice. "Breslin, by all means, for the one you were sure of. But the second man, the one you had hopes of—who should that be but me? I thank you. I am touched. I am myself indifferent honest, as Shakespeare puts it."[41]

The sheriff licked his dry lips.

"If you think I am going to stay here to be insulted—"

"You are!" taunted John Wesley Pringle. "You'll stay right here. What? Leave me here to tell what I have to say to an honest man and a half? Impossible! You'll not let me out of your sight."

"My amateur Ananias,"[42] interrupted Anastacio dispassionately, "you are, unintentionally, perhaps, doing me half of a grave injustice. In this particular instance—for this day and date only—I am as pure as a new-mown hay. To prevent all misapprehension let me say now that I never thought Foy killed Dick Marr."

"In heaven's name, why?" demanded Breslin.

"My honest but thick-skulled friend, let me put in my oar," implored the Major. "Let me show you that Matt Lisner never thought Foy was guilty. Foy said last night, before the killing, that he was coming up here, didn't he?"

---

41 Hamlet advises Ophelia in act 3, scene 1, to "get thee to a nunnery," then adds that "I am myself indifferent honest."

42 Ananias of Damascus restored the sight of Saul (a.k.a. St. Paul) and was one of the seventy disciples of Christ mentioned in Luke and Acts.

"Hey, Major—hold up!" cried Pringle. But Vorhis was not to be stopped.

"Don't you see, you doddering imbecile? If Foy had really killed Dick Marr he might have gone to any other place in the world—but he wouldn't have come here."

"Aha! So Foy did come here, hey?" croaked the sheriff, triumphant in his turn. "Thanks, Major, for the information, though I was sure before, humanly speaking, that he came this way."

"Which is another way of saying that you don't think Foy did the killing—that you don't even suspect him of it," said Anastacio. As the Major subsided, crestfallen. "Matt Lisner, I know that you hate Foy. I know that you welcome this chance to get rid of him. Make no mistake, Breslin. I was not wanted here. I wasn't asked and none of my people were brought along. I tagged along, though—to wait. It's one of the best little things I do—waiting. And I came to protect Foy, not to capture him. I came to keep right at his side, in case he surrendered without a fight—for fear he might be killed . . . escaping . . . on the way back. It's a way that we have in Las Uvas!"

Lisner threw a look of hate at his deputy.

"You don't mean to tell me there's any danger of anything like that?" said Breslin, staggered and aghast.

"Every danger. That's an old gag—the *ley fuga*."[43]

"You lie!" bawled Creagan. His six-shooter covered Anastacio.

"That'll keep. Put up your gun, Bennie," said Anastacio with great composure. "Supper's most ready. Besides, the Barelas won't like it if you shoot me this way. There's a lot of the Barelas, Ben. I'll tell you what I'll do, though—I'll slip the idea to my crowd, and any time you want to kill me on an even break, no Barela or Ascarate will take it up. Put it right in your little holster—put it up, I say! That's right. You see, Breslin? Don't let Foy out of your sight if he should be taken."

"But he'll never let himself be taken alive," said Vorhis. "Even if anyone wants to take him—alive. Pass the word to your friends, Breslin, unless you want them to take part in a deliberate, foreplanned murder."

---

43 escape from the law

"Damn you, what do you mean?" shouted the sheriff.

"By God, sir, I mean just what I say!"

"Why, girls!" said Pringle. "You shock me! This is most unladylike. This is scandalous talk. Be nice! Please—pretty please! See, here comes some more pussy-foot posse—three, six, eleven hungry men. Have they got Foy? No; they have not got Foy. Is he up? He is up. Look who's here too! Good old Applegate and Brother Espalin. I wonder now if they're goin' to give me the cut direct, like Creagan did? You notice, Mr. Breslin."

The horsemen rode into the corral.

"No; don't go, Sheriff," said Anastacio.

"I'm anxious to see if those two will recognize Ananias the Amateur. They'll be here directly. You, either, Creagan. Else I'll shoot you both in the back, accidentally, cleaning my gun."

From without was the sound of spurred feet in haste; three men appeared at the open door.

"Why, if it ain't George! Good old George!" cried Pringle, rising with outstretched arms. "And my dear friend Espalin! What a charming reunion!"

Applegate's eyes threw a startled question at his chief and at Creagan; Espalin slipped swiftly back through the door.

"I don't know you, sir," said Applegate.

"George! You're never going to disown me! Joe's gone, too. Nobody loves me!"

The third man, a grizzled and bristly old warrior with a limp, broke in with a roar.

"What in hell's going on here?" he stormed.

"You are, for one thing, if you don't moderate your voice," said Anastacio. "Nueces, you bellow like the bulls of Bashan.[44] Mr. Applegate, meet Mr. Pringle."

"What does he mean, then, by such monkeyshines?" demanded the other—old Nueces River, chief of police, ex-ranger, and, for this occasion,

44 Psalms 22:12: "Many bulls have compassed me: strong bulls of Bashan have beset me round."

deputy sheriff. "I got no time for foolishness. And you can't run no whizzer on me, Barela. Don't you try it!"

"Oh, they're just joking, Nueces," said the Major. "Tell us how about it. Here, I'll light the lamp; it's getting dark. Find any sign of Foy?"

Nueces leveled a belligerent finger at the Major.

"You've been joking, too! I've heard about you. Lisner, I'm ashamed of you! Let Vorhis pull the wool over your eyes, while you sit here and jaw all afternoon, doing nothing!"

"Why, what did you find out?"

"A-plenty. Them stiffs you sent out found Foy's horse, to begin with."

"Sure it was Foy's horse?" queried Lisner eagerly.

"Sure! I know the horse—that big calico horse of his."

"Why didn't you follow him up?"

"Follow hell! Oh, some of the silly fools are milling round out there—going over to the San Andrés to-night to take a big hunt *mañana*. Not me. That horse was a blind. They pottered round tryin' to find some trace of Foy—blind fools!—till I met up with 'em. I'd done gathered in that mizzable red-headed Joe Cowan on a give-out horse, claim-in' he'd been chousin' after broom-tails. He'd planted Foy's horse, I reckon. But it can't be proved, so I let him go. He'll have to walk in; that's one good thing."

"But Foy—where do you figure Foy's gone?"

"Maybe he simply was not," suggested Pringle, "like Enoch when he was translated into all European languages, including the Scandinavian."[45]

"Pringle, if you say another word I'll have you gagged!" said the exasperated sheriff. "Don't you reckon, Nueces, that Cowan brought Foy a barefooted horse? He can't have gone on afoot or you'd have seen his tracks."

"Sheriff, you certainly are an easy mark!" returned Nueces, in great disgust. "Foy didn't go on afoot or horseback, because he was never there. I've told you twice: Cowan left that calico horse on purpose for us to find. Vorhis is Foy's friend. Can't you see, if Foy had tried to get away by hard riding he

45 The apocryphal book of Enoch was published in Swedish translation under the title *Henoks bok* in 1901.

would have had a fresh horse, not the one he rode from Las Uvas, and you wouldn't have found a penful of fresh horses to chase him with? Not in a thousand years! That was to make it nice and easy for you to ride on—a six-year-old kid could see through it! It's a wonder you didn't all fall for it and chase away. No, sir! Foy either stopped down on the river and sent his horse on to fool us—or, more likely, he's up in the Buttes. Did you look there?"

"I sent the boys round to out sign. I didn't feel justified in hunting out the rough places till we had more men. Too much cover for him."

"And none for you, I s'pose? Mamma! but you're a fine sheriff! Look now: After we started back here we sighted a dust comin' 'way up north. We went over, and 'twas Hargis, the Major's buckaroo, throwin' in a bunch from the round-up. He didn't know nothin' and was not right sure of that—till I mentioned your reward. Soon as ever I mentioned twenty-five hundred, he loosened up right smart."

"Well? Did he know where Foy was?"

"No; but he knew of the place where I judge Foy is, this very yet. Gosh!" said Nueces River in deep disgust, "it beats hell what men will do for a little dirty money! Seems there's a cave near the top of the least of them two buttes—the roughest one—a cave with two mouths, one right on the big top. Nobody much knows where it is, only the V H outfit."

Pringle had edged across the room. He now plucked at Bell Applegate's sleeve.

"Say, is that right about that reward—twenty-five hundred?" he whispered. His eyes glistened.

"Forty-five," said Bell behind his hand. "The Masons,[46] they put up a thousand, and Dick's old uncle—that would have let Dick starve or work—he tacked on a thousand more. Dead or alive!" He looked down at Pringle's face, at Pringle's working fingers, opening and shutting avariciously; he sneered. "Don't you wish you may get it? S-sh! Hear what the old man's saying."

---

46 Soon after Fountain, who was a Freemason, and his son disappeared, the Aztec Masonic Lodge in Las Cruces offered an additional reward for the return of their bodies and information leading to the arrest and conviction of their abductors. See also Hutchinson, 61, 132.

During the whispered colloquy the old ranger had kept on:

"There's where he is, a twenty-to-one shot! He'll lay quiet, likely, thinkin' we'll miss him. Brush growin' over both the cave mouths, Hargis says, so you might pass right by if you didn't know where to look. These short nights he couldn't never get clear on foot. Thirty mile to the next water—we'd find his tracks and catch him. But he might make a break to get away, at that. Never can tell about a he-man like that. We can't take no chances. We'll pick a bite of supper and then we surround that hill, quiet as mice, and close up on him. He can't see us to shoot if we're fool enough to make any noise. Come daylight, we'll have him cornered, every man behind a bowlder. If he shows up he's our meat; if he don't we'll starve him out."

"And suppose he isn't there?" said Creagan. "What would we look like, watching an empty cave two or three days?"

"What do we look like now? Give you three guesses," retorted Nueces.

"And how'd we look rushin' that empty cave if it didn't happen to be empty? Excuse me! I'd druther get three grand heehaws and a tiger for bein' ridiculous than to have folks tiptoe by a-whisperin': 'How natural he looks!' I been a pretty tough old bird in my day—but goin' up a tunnel after Kitty Foy ain't my idea of foresight."

"Some man—some good man, too—will have to stay here and stand guard on the Major and this fresh guy, Pringle," said the sheriff thoughtfully. "He'll get his slice of the money, of course."

"You'll find a many glad to take that end of the job; for," said Nueces River, "it is in my wise old noddle some of us are going to be festerin' in Abraham's bosom[47] before we earn that reward money. Leave Applegate—he's in bad shape for climbing anyway; bruise on his belly big as a wash-pan."

"Bronc' bucked me over on the saddle horn," explained Applegate. "Sure, I'll stay. And the Pringle person will be right here when you get back, too."

"Let the Major take some supper in to Miss Vorhis," suggested Breslin.

47 where the righteous dead may be comforted.

"I'll keep an eye on him. He can eat with her and cheer her up a little. This is hard lines for a girl."

Lisner shrugged his shoulders.

"We have to keep her here till Foy's caught. She might bring a sight of trouble down on us."

"Say, what's the matter with me going out and eating a few?" asked Pringle.

"You stay here! You talk too much with your mouth," replied the sheriff. "I'll send in a snack for you and Bell. Come on, boys."

They filed out to the cook's fire in the walled courtyard.

"George, dear," said Pringle when the two were left alone, "is that right about the reward? 'Cause I sure want to get in on it."

"Damn likely. You knew where Foy was. You know where he is now. Why didn't you tell us, if you wanted in on the reward?"

"Why, George, I didn't know there was any reward. Besides, him and me split up as soon as we got clear of town."

"You're a damn liar!"

"That's what the sheriff said. Somebody must 'a' give me away," complained John Wesley. He rolled a cigarette and walked to the table. "All the same, you're making a mistake. You hadn't ought to roil me. Just for that, soon as they're all off on their man hunt, I'm goin' to study up some scheme to get away."

"I got a picture of you gettin' away!"

"George," said John Wesley, "you see that front door? Well, that's what we call in theatrical circles a practical door. Along toward morning I'm going out through that practical door. You'll see!"

He raised the lamp, held the cigarette over the chimney top and puffed till he got a light; so doing he smoked the chimney. To inspect the damage he raised the lamp higher. Swifter than thought he hurled it at his warder's head. The blazing lamp struck Applegate between the eyes. Pringle's fist flashed up and smote him grievously under the jaw; he fell crashing; the half-drawn gun clattered from his slackened fingers. Pringle caught it up and plunged into the dark through the practical door.

He ran down the adobe wall of the water pen; a bullet whizzed by; he turned the corner; he whisked over the wall, back into the water pen. Shouts, curses, the sound of rushing feet without the wall. Pringle crouched in the deep shadow of the wall, groped his way to the long row of watering troughs, and wormed himself under the upper trough, where the creaking windmill and the splashing of water from the supply pipe would drown out the sound of his labored breath.

Horsemen boiled from the yard gate with uproar and hullabaloo; Pringle heard their shouts; he saw the glare of soap weeds, fired to help their search.

The lights died away; the shouts grew fainter: they swelled again as the searchers straggled back, vociferous. Pringle caught scraps of talk as they watered their horses.

"Clean getaway!"

"One bad actor, that *hombre*!"

"Regular Go-Getter!"

"Batting average about thirteen hundred, I should figger."

"Life-size he-man! Where do you suppose—"

"Saw a lad make just such another break once in Van Zandt County—"[48]

"Say! Who're you crowdin'?"

"Hi, fellers! Bill's giving some more history of the state of Van Zandt!"

"Applegate's pretty bad hurt."

"—in a gopher hole and near broke my fool neck."

"Where'd this old geezer come from, anyway? Never heard of him before!"

"'Tain't fair, just when we was all crowdin' up for supper! He might have waited."

"This will be merry hell and repeat if he hooks up with Foy," said Creagan's voice, adding a vivid description of Pringle.

Old Nueces answered, raising his voice:

"He's afoot. We got to beat him to it. Let's ride!"

"That's right," said the sheriff. "But we'll grab something to eat first.

48 A county in northeast Texas.

Saddle up, Hargis, and lead us to your little old cave. Robbins,[49] while we snatch a bite you bunch what canteens we've got and fill 'em up. Then you watch the old man and that girl, and let Breslin come with us. You can eat after we've gone."

"Don't let the girl heave a pillow at you, Robbins!" warned a voice.

"Better not stop to eat," urged Nueces.

"We can lope up and get to the foot of Thumb Butte before Pringle gets halfway—if he's going there at all. Most likely he's had a hand in the Marr killing and is just running away to save his own precious neck," said the sheriff. "We'll scatter out around the hill when we get to the roughs, and go up afoot till every man can see or hear his neighbor, so Pringle can't get through. Then we'll wait till daylight."

"That may suit you," retorted Nueces. "Me, I don't intend for any man that will buck a gun with a lamp to throw in with Kit Foy while I stuff my paunch. That sort is just the build to do a mile in nothing flat—and it's only three miles to the hill. I'm goin' now, and I'm goin' hellity-larrup! Come on, anybody with more brains than belly—I'm off to light a line of soap weeds on that hill so this Mr. Pringle-With-the-Punch don't walk himself by. If he wants up he'll have to hoof it around the other side of the hill. We won't make any light on the north side. That Bar Cross outfit is too damn inquisitive. The night herders would see it; they'd smell trouble; and like as not the whole bilin' of 'em would come pryin' down here by daylight. Guess they haven't heard about Foy or they'd be here now. They're strong for Foy. Come on, you waddies!"

Mr. Pringle-with-the-Punch, squeezed, cramped, and muddy under the trough, heard this supperless plan with displeasure; his hope had been otherwise. He heard the sound of hurried mounting; from the thunder of galloping hoofs it would seem that a goodly number of the posse had come up to the specifications laid down by the old ranger.

The others clanked away, leaving their horses standing. The man Robbins grumbled from saddle to saddle and gathered canteens. As he filled them from the supply pipe directly above Mr. Pringle's head, he set them

49 W. M. Robbins, sheriff of Sierra County in 1902.

on the ground within easy reach of Mr. Pringle's hand. Acting on this hint Mr. Pringle's hand withdrew a canteen, quite unostentatiously. An unnecessary precaution, as it turned out; Mr. Robbins, having filled that batch, went to the horses farther down the troughs to look for more canteens. So Pringle wriggled out with his canteen, selected a horse, and rode quietly through the open gate.

"Going already?" called Robbins as he passed.

Secure under cover of darkness, Pringle answered in the voice of one who, riding, eats:

"Yes, indeedy; I ain't no hawg. Wasn't much hungry nohow!"

CHAPTER V

AT THE FOOT OF Little Thumb Butte a lengthening semicircle of fire flared through the night. John Wesley Pringle swung far out on the plain to circle round it.

"This takes time," he muttered to himself, "but at least I know where not to go. That old rip-snorter sure put a spoke in my wheel! Looks like Foy might see them lights and drift out away from this. But he won't, I guess—they said his hidey-hole was right on top, and the shoulder of the hill will hide the fires from him. Probably asleep, anyhow, thinkin' he's safe. I slep' three hours this morning at the Major's; but Foy he didn't sleep any. Even if he did leave, they'd track him up in the morning and get him—and he knows it. Somebody's goin' to be awfully annoyed when he misses this horse."

He could see the riders, dim-flitting as they passed between him and the flames. Once he stopped to listen; he heard the remaining half of the man-hunt leaving the ranch. They were riding hard. Thereafter Pringle had no mercy on his horse. Ride as he might, those who followed had the inner circle; when he rounded the fires and struck the hill his start was perilously slight. While the footing was soft he urged the wearied horse up the slope; at the first rocky space he abandoned the poor beast lest the floundering of shod hoofs should betray him. He took off saddle and bridle; he hung the canteen over his shoulder and pressed on afoot.

A light breeze had overcast the stars with thin and fleecy clouds. This made for Pringle's safety; it also made the going harder—and it would have been hard going by daylight.

The slope became steeper; ledges of rock, little at first, became larger and more frequent; he came to bluffs that barred his progress, slow and painful at best; he was forced to search to left or right for broken places where he could climb. Bits of rock, dislodged by his feet, fell clattering despite his utmost care; he heard the like from below, to the left, to the right. The short night wore swiftly on.

With equal fortune John Wesley should have maintained his lead. But he found more than his share of no-thoroughfares. Before long his ears told him that men were almost abreast of him on each side. He was handicapped now, because he must shun any chance meeting. His immediate neighbors, however, had no such fear; they edged closer and closer together as they climbed. At last, stopped against a perpendicular wall ten feet high, he heard them creeping toward him from both sides, with a guarded "Coo-ee!" each to the other; John Wesley slipped down the hill to the nearest bush. His neighbors came together and held a whispered discourse. They viewed the barrier with marked patience, it seemed; they sat down in friendly fashion and smoked cigarette after cigarette; the hum of their hushed voices reached Pringle, murmuring and indistinct. It might almost be thought that they were willing for others to precede them in the place of honor. A faint glow showed in the east; the moon had thoughts of rising.

After an interminable half-hour the two worthies passed on to the right. Pringle took to the left, more swiftly. Time for caution had passed; moonlight might betray him. When he found a way up that unlucky wall others of the search party farther to the left were well beyond him.

Perhaps a quarter of a mile away, the last sheer cliff, the Thumb which gave the hill its name, frowned above him, a hundred feet from base to crest. Pringle bore obliquely up to the right. Speed was his best safety now; he pushed on boldly, cheered by the thought that if seen by any of the posse he would be taken for one of their own number. But Foy, seeing him, would make the same mistake! It was an uncomfortable reflection.

The pitch was less abrupt now, and there were no more ledges; instead, bowlders were strewn along the rounded slope, with bush and stunted tree between. Through these Pringle breasted his way, seeking even more to protect himself from above than from below, forced at times to crawl through an open space exposed to possible fire from both sides; so came at last to the masses of splintered and broken rock at the foot of the cliff, where he sank breathless and panting.

The tethered constellations paled in the sky; the moon rose and lit the cliff with silver fire. The worst was yet to come. Foy would ask no questions of any prowler, that was sure; he would reason that a friend would call out boldly. And John Wesley had no idea where Foy or his cave might be. Yet he must be found.

With a hearty swig at the canteen Pringle crept off to the right. The moonlight beat full upon the cliff. He had little trouble in that ruin of broken stone to find cover from foes below; but at each turn he confidently looked forward to a bullet from his friend.

"Foy! Foy!" he called softly as he crawled. "It's Pringle! Don't shoot!"

After a space he came to an angle where the cliff turned abruptly west and dwindled sharply in height. He remembered what the Major had said—the upper entrance of the cave came out on the highest crest of the hill. He turned back to retrace his painful way. The smell of dawn was in the air; the east sparkled. No sound came from the ambush all around. The end was near.

He passed by his starting-point; he crept on by slide and bush and stone. The moon magic faded and paled, mingled with the swift gray of dawn. He held his perilous way. Cold sweat stood on his brow. If Foy or a foe of Foy were on the cliff now, how easy to topple down a stone upon him! The absolute stillness was painful. A thought came to him of Stella Vorhis—her laughing eyes, her misty hair, the little hand that had lingered upon his own. Such a little, little hand!

Before him a narrow slit opened in the wall—such a crevice as the Major had described.

"Foy! Oh, Foy!" he called. No answer came. He raised his voice a little louder. "Foy! Speak if you're there! It's Pringle!"

A gentle voice answered from the cleft:

"Let us hope, for your sake, that you are not mistaken about that. I should be dreadfully vexed if you were deceiving me. The voice is the voice of Pringle, but how about the face? I can only see your back."

"I would raise my head, so you could take a nice look by the well-known cold gray light of the justly celebrated dawn," rejoined Pringle, "if I wasn't reasonably sure that a rifle shot would promptly mar the classic outlines of my face. They're all around you, Foy. Hargis, he gave you away. Don't show a finger nail of yourself. Let me crawl up behind that big rock ahead and then you can identify me."

"It's you, all right," said Foy when Pringle reached the rock and straightened himself up.

"I told you so," said Pringle, peering into the shadows of the cleft. "I can't see you. And how am I going to get to you? There are twenty men with point-blank range. I'm muddy, scratched, bruised, tired and hungry, sleepy and cross—and there's thirty feet in the open between here and you, and it nearly broad daylight. If I try to cross that I'll run twenty-five hundred pounds to the ton, pure lead. Well, we can put up a pretty nifty fight, even so. You go back to the other outlet of your cave and I'll stay here. I'm kinder lonesome, too. . . . Toss me some cartridges first. I only got five. I left in a hurry. You got forty-fives?"

"Plenty. But you can't stay there. They'll pot you from the top of the bluff, first off. Besides, you got a canteen, I see. You back up to that mountain mahogany bush, slip under it, and worm down through the rocks till you come to a little scrub-oak tree and a big granite bowlder. They'll give you shelter to cross the ridge into a deep ravine that leads here where I am. You'll be out of sight all the way up once you hit the ravine. I'd—I'd worm along pretty spry if I was you, going down as far as the scrub oak—say, about as swift as a rattlesnake strikes—and pray any little prayers you happen to remember. And say, Pringle, before you go . . . I'm rather obliged to you for coming up here; risking taking cold and all. If it'll cheer you up any I'll undertake that anyone getting you on the trip will think there's one gosh-awful echo here."

"S'long!" said Pringle.

He wriggled backward and disappeared.

Ten minutes later he writhed under the bush at Foy's feet.

"Never saw me!" he said. "But I'll always sleep in coils after this—always supposing we got any after this coming to us."

"One more crawl," said Foy, leading the way. "We'll go up on top. Regular fort up there. If we've got to die we'll die in the sun."

He stooped at what seemed the end of the passage and crawled out of sight under the low branches of a stunted cedar. Pringle followed and found himself in the pitch dark.

"Grab hold of my coat tail. I know my way, feeling the wall. Watch your step or you'll bark your shins."

The cave floor was smooth underfoot, except for scattered rocks; it rose and dipped, but the general trend was sharply upward.

"You're quite an institution, Pringle. You've made good Stella's word of you—the best ever!" said Foy as they mounted. "But you can't do me any good, really. I'll enjoy your company, but I wish you hadn't come."

"That's all right. I always like to finish what I begin."

"Well," remarked Foy cheerfully, "I reckon we've reached the big finish, both of us. I don't see any way out. All they've got to do is to sit tight till we starve out for water. Wish you was out of it. It's going to be tough on Stella, losing her friend and—and me, both at once. How's she making out? Full of fight and hope to the last, I'll bet."

"They had me under herd; but she was wishing for the Bar Cross buddies to butt in, I believe. Reckon your sheriff-man guessed it. He had her under guard, too."

"Nice man, the sheriff! How'd you get away from your herder?"

"He don't just remember," said Pringle.

"Who was it?"

"Applegate. Dreadful absent-minded, Applegate is. Ouch! There went my other shin. Had any sleep?"

"Most all night. Something woke me up about two hours ago, and I kept on the look-out ever since."

"That was me, I guess. I had to step lively. They was crowding me."

"If the Bar Cross happened to get word," observed Foy thoughtfully, "we might stand some hack. But they won't. It's good-by, vain world, for ours! Say, in case a miracle happens for you, just make a memo about the sheriff being a nuisance, will you?"

"I'll tie a string on my finger. Anything else?"

"You might stick around and cheer Stella up a little. I'll do as much for you sometime. I'm thinking she'll feel pretty bad at first. Here we are!"

A faint glimmer showed ahead. They crawled under low bushes and stumbled out, in what seemed at first a dazzle of light; into a small saucer-shaped plat of earth a few feet across, enclosed by an irregular oval made by great blocks of stone, man-high. Below, a succession of little cliffs fell away, stair fashion, to an exceeding high and narrow gap which separated Little Thumb Butte from its greater neighbor, Big Thumb Butte.

"Castle Craney Crow,"[50] smiled Foy with a proprietary wave of his hand. "Just right for our business, isn't it? Make yourself at home, while I take a peep around about." He bent to peer through bush and crack. "Nothing stirring," he announced. He leaned his rifle against a walling rock. "Let's have a look at that water."

He raised the canteen to his lips. Pringle struck swift and hard to the tilted chin. Foy dropped like a poled bullock; his head struck heavily against the sharp corner of a rock. Pringle pounced on the stricken man. He threw Foy's six-shooter aside; he pulled Foy's wrists behind him and tied them tightly with a handkerchief. Then he rolled his captive over.

Foy's eyes opened; they rolled back till only the whites were visible; his lips twitched. Pringle hastily bound his handkerchief to the gash the stone had made; he sprinkled the blood-streaked face with water; he spilled drops of water between the parted lips. Foy did not revive. Pringle stuck his hat on the rifle muzzle and waved it over the parapet of rock.

"Hello!" he shouted. "Bring on your reward! I've got Foy! It's me—Pringle! Come get him; and be quick—he's bleeding mighty bad."

"Come out, you! Hands up and no monkey business!" answered a startled voice not fifty yards away.

---

50 *Castle Craneycrow* (1902) by the American novelist George Barr McCutcheon (1866–1928).

“Who’s that? That you, Nueces? Give me your word and I’ll lug him out. No time to lose—he’s hurt, and hurt bad.”

“You play fair and we will. I give my word!” shouted Nueces.

“Here goes!” Pringle pitched the rifle over. A moment later he staggered out between the rocks, bearing Foy’s heavy weight in his arms. The head hung helpless, blood-spattered; the body was limp and slack; the legs dragged sprawling; the dreaded hands were bound.

Pringle laid his burden on the grass.

“Here he is, you hyenas! His hands are tied—are you still afraid of him? Damn you! The man’s bleeding to death!”

CHAPTER VI

"YOU TREACHEROUS, DIRTY HOUND!" said Breslin.

"Of all the low-down skunks I ever seen, you sure are the skunkiest!" said Nueces. "The sheriff was right after all. Cur-dog fits you to a T." He finished washing out the cut on Foy's head as he spoke. "Now the bandages, Anastacio. We'll have the blood stopped in a jiffy. Funny he hasn't come to. It's been a long while. It ain't the head ails him. This isn't such a deep cut; it oughtn't to put him out. Just happened to strike a vein." He bound up the cut with the deftness of experience.

"I hit him under the jaw," observed Pringle. "That's what did the business for him. He'll be around directly."

Anastacio looked up at Pringle; measureless contempt was in his eyes.

"Judas Iscariot[51] could have sublet his job to you at half price if you'd been in the neighborhood. You are the limit, plus! I hope to see you fry in a New English hell!"

"Oh, that's all right, too," said Pringle unabashed. "I might just as well have that forty-five hundred as anyone. It wouldn't amount to much split amongst all you fellows, but it's quite a bundle for one man. That'll keep the wolf from the well-known door for quite a while."

"You won't touch a cent of it!" declared the sheriff.

"Won't I though? We'll see about that. I captured him alone, didn't I? Oh, I reckon I'll finger the money, alrighty!"

51 The disciple Judas Iscariot betrayed Christ in return for thirty pieces of silver.

"Here, fellows; give him a bait of whisky," said Creagan.

Breslin, kneeling at Foy's side, took the extended flask. They administered the stimulant cautiously, a sip at a time. Foy's eyes flickered; his breath came freer.

"He's coming!" said Breslin. "Give him a sip of water now."

"He'll be O.K. in five minutes, far as settin' up goes," said old Nueces, well pleased; "but he ain't goin' to be any too peart for quite some time—not for gettin' down off o' this hill. See—he's battin' his eyes and working his hands around. He sure heard the birdies sing!"

"The rest of you boys had just as well go on down to the shack," directed the sheriff. "Creagan and Joe and me will take care of Foy till he's able to move or be moved, and bring him into camp. You just lead up our three horses and an extra one for Foy—up as far as you can fetch 'em. One of you can ride home behind someone. Call down to the bunch under the cliff that we've got 'em, and for them to hike out to the ranch and take a nap. You'd better turn old Vorhis loose—and that girl. They can't do any harm now."

"Bring my horse, too," said Anastacio. "I'm staying. I want to be sure the invalid gets . . . proper care."

"Me too," said Breslin.

"And I'm staying to kinder superintend," said Nueces dryly. "Sheriff," he added, as the main body of the posse fell off down the hill—"and you, too, Barela—I don't just know what's going on here, but I'm stayin' with you to a fare-you-well. You two seem to be bucking each other."

No one answered.

"Sulky, hey? Well, anyhow, call it off long enough to drive this Pringle thing away from here. He ain't fittin' for no man to herd with."

"I'm staying right with this man Foy till I get that reward," announced Pringle. "Those are my superintentions. Much I care what you think about me! There's other places besides this."

Breslin raised his eye from Foy's face and regarded Pringle without heat—a steady, contemplative look, as of one who studies some strange and interesting animal. Then he waved his hand down the pass, where certain of the departing posse, were bringing the saddle horses in obedience to the sheriff's instructions.

"They'll carry a nice report of you," observed Breslin quietly. "What do you suppose that little girl will think?"

A flicker of red came to Pringle's hard brown face. Even the scorn of Espalin and Creagan had left him unabashed, but now he winced visibly; and, for once, he had no reply to make.

Foy gasped, struggled to a sitting position, aided by his oddly assorted ministrants, gazed round in a dazed condition and lapsed back into unconsciousness.

"I'll take my dyin' oath it ain't the cut that ails him," said the ranger, tucking a coat under Foy's blood-stained head. "That must have been a horrible jolt on his jaw, Pringle. You're no kind of a man at all—no part of a man. You're a shameless, black-hearted traitor; but I got to hand it to you as a slugger. Two knock-outs in one day—and such men as them! I don't understand it."

"He 'most keel Applegate," said the Mexican.

"Aw, it's easy!" said Pringle eagerly. "There ain't one man in a thousand knows how to fight. It ain't cussin' and gritting your teeth, and swellin' up your biceps and clenching your fists up tight that does the trick. You want to hit like there wasn't anybody there. I'll show you sometime."

He paused inquiringly, as if to book any acceptance of this kindly offer. No such engagements being made, Pringle continued:

"Supposin' you was throwin' a baseball[52] and your hand struck a man accidentally; you'd hurt him every time—only you'd break your arm that way. That ain't the way to strike. I'll show you."

"That wasn't no olive branch I was holdin' out," stated Nueces River.

"You'll show me nothin'—turncoat!"

"It helps a lot, too, when the man you hit is not expecting it," suggested Anastacio smoothly. "You might show me sometime—when I'm looking for it."

"Now what's biting you?" demanded Pringle testily. "What did you expect me to do—send 'em a note by registered mail?"

"I'm not speaking about Applegate. That was all right. I am speaking about your friend."

---

52 Rhodes was an avid baseball player and fan.

"Here; Kit's coming to life again," said Lisner.

Kitty Foy rolled over; they propped him up; he looked round rather wildly from one to the other. His face cleared. His eye fell upon Pringle, where it rested with a steady intentness. When he spoke, at last, he ignored the others entirely.

"And I thought you were my friend, Pringle. I trusted you!" he said with ominous quietness. "I'll make a note of it. I have a good memory, Pringle—and good friends. Give me some water, someone. I feel sick."

Espalin brought a canteen.

"Take your time, Chris," said Lisner. "Tell us when you feel able to go."

"I'll be all right after a little. Say, boys, it was the queerest feeling—coming to, I mean. I could almost hear your voices, first. Then I heard them a long ways off but I couldn't make any sense to the words. Here; let me lean my back up against this rock and sit quiet for a while. Then we'll go. I'm giddy yet."

"I've got it!" announced Nueces a moment later. "Barela, he's hankering to be sheriff—that's the trouble. He wanted to take Chris himself, to help things along. That would be quite a feather in any man's hat—done fair. And the sheriff, natural enough, he don't want nothing of the kind."

"That's it," said Anastacio, amusement in his eyes. "I knew you were a good gunman, Nueces, but I never suspected you of brains before."

"What's the matter with that guess?" said Nueces sulkily. "Kid, you're always ridin' me. Don't you try to use any spurs!"

"I'm in on that," said Pringle, rising brightly. "That's my happy chance to join in this lovin' conversation. Speaking about gunmen, I'm a beaut! See that hawk screechin' around up there? Well, watch!"

The hawk soared high above. Pringle barely raised Foy's rifle to his shoulder as he fired; the hawk tumbled headlong. Pringle jerked the lever, throwing another cartridge into the barrel, as if to fire again at the falling bird. Inconceivably swift, the cocked rifle whirled to cover the seated posse.

"Steady!" said Pringle. "I'm watchin' you, Nueces! Chris, when you're able to walk, go on down and pick you a horse from that bunch. Unsaddle the others and drive 'em along a ways as you go." Still speaking, he edged behind the cover of a high rock. "I'll address the meetin' till you get a good head start. . . . Steady in the boat!"

"Well, by Heck!" said Nueces.

"And I thought you had betrayed me!" cried Foy.

"Well, I hadn't. This was the only show to get off. . . . I hate to kill you, Nueces; but I will if you make a move."

"Hell! I ain't makin' no move! What do you think I am—a damn fool?" said Nueces. "If I moved any it was because I am about to crack under the justly celebrated strain. Say, young fellow, it strikes me that you change sides pretty often."

"Yes; I am the Acrobat of the Breakfast Table,"[53] said Pringle modestly. "Thanks for the young fellow. That listens good."

"Look out I don't have you performing on a tight rope yet!" growled the sheriff hoarsely. "There'll be more to this. You haven't got out of the country yet."

"That will be all from you, Sheriff. You, too, Creagan—and Espalin. Not a word or I'll shoot. And I don't care how soon you begin to talk. That goes!"

Espalin shriveled up; the sheriff and Creagan sat sullen and silent.

Foy got to his feet rather unsteadily.

"Chris, you might slip around and gather up their guns," said Pringle. "Pick out one for yourself. I left yours where I threw it when I picked it out of your belt. I meant to knock you out, Chris—there wasn't any other way; but I didn't mean to plumb kill you. You hit your head on a rock when you fell. It wouldn't have done any good to have got the drop on you. You had made up your mind not to surrender. You would have shot anyhow; and, of course, I couldn't shoot. I'd just have got myself killed for nothing. No good to play I'd taken you prisoner. This crowd knew you wouldn't be taken—except by treachery. So I played traitor. As it was, when I knocked you out you didn't look much like no put-up job. You was bleeding like a stuck pig."

53 Pringle puns on the title of Oliver Wendell Holmes' essay collection *The Autocrat of the Breakfast Table* (1858). According to Sonnichsen, *The Autocrat* was Rhodes' "favorite book" (208).

"Hold on, there, before you try to take my gun!" warned old Nueces River as Foy came to him for his gun, collecting. "You got the big drop on me, Pringle, and I wouldn't raise a hand to keep Chris from getting off anyhow—not now. But I used to be a ranger—and the rangers were sworn never to give up their guns."

"How about it, Pringle?" asked Foy, who had already relieved the sheriff and his satellites of their guns. "He'll do exactly as he says—both ways."

"I wasn't done talking yet," said Nueces irritably. "But I'll let Chris take my gun, on one condition."

"What's that?" inquired Pringle.

"Why, if you ain't busy next Saturday I'd like to have you call around—about one o'clock, say—and kick me good and hard."

"Let him keep his gun. He called me a young fellow. And I don't want Breslin's, anyway. He's all right. Not to play any favorites, let Anastacio keep his. There are times," said Pringle, "when I have great hopes of Anastacio. I'm thinking some of taking him in hand to see if I can't make a man of him."

"Ananias the Amateur," said Anastacio, "I thank you for those kind words. And I'd like to see you Saturday about two—when you get through with Nueces. I'm next on the waiting list. This will be a lesson to me never to let my opinion of a man be changed by anything he may do."

"If you fellows feel that way," said Foy, "how about me? How do you suppose I feel? This man has risked his life fifty times for me—and what did I think of him?"

"If you ask me, Christopher," said Anastacio, "I think you were quite excusable. It was all very well to dissemble his love—but I should feel doubtful of any man that handed me such a wallop as that until the matter had been fully explained."

"What I want to know, Pringle, is, how the deuce you got up here so slick?" said Nueces.

"Oh, that's easy! I can run a mile in nothing flat."

"Oh—that's it? You hid in the water pen?"

"Under the troughs. Bright idea of yours, them fires! I knew just where not to go. After you left I hooked a horse. If you'd had sense enough to go with the sheriff and eat your supper like a human being I'd 'a' hooked two horses, and Chris and me would now be getting farther and farther. I don't want you ever to do that again. Suppose Chris had killed me when I tried to knock him out? Fine large name I would 'a' left for myself, wouldn't I?"

"If you had fought it out with us," said Breslin musingly, "you would have been killed—both of you; and you would have killed others. Mr. Pringle, you have done a fine thing. I apologize to you."

"Why, that all goes without saying, my boy. As for my part—why, I don't bother much about a blue tin heaven or a comic-supplement hell, but I'm right smart interested in right here and now. It's a right nice little old world, take it by and large, and I like to help out at whatever comes my way, if it takes fourteen innings. But, so long as you feel that way about it, maybe you'll believe me now, when I say that Christopher Foy was with me all last night and he didn't shoot Dick Marr."

"That's right," said Foy. "I don't know who killed Dick Marr; but I do know that Creagan, Joe Espalin, and Applegate intended to kill me last night. They gave me back my six-shooter, that Ben Creagan had borrowed—and it was loaded with blanks. Then they pitched onto me, and if it hadn't been for Pringle they'd have got me sure! We left town at eleven o'clock and rode straight to the Vorhis Ranch."

"I believe you," said Anastacio. "You skip along now, Chris. You're fit to ride."

"Why shouldn't I stay and see it out?"

"It won't do. For one thing, your thinker isn't working as per invoice," said Nueces River. "You're in no fix to do yourself justice. We'll look after your interests. You know some of the posse might be coming back, askin' fool questions. Pull your freight up to the Bar Cross till we send for you."

"Well—if you think Pringle isn't running any risks I'll go."

"We'll take care of Pringle. Guess we'll make him sheriff next fall, maybe—just to keep Anastacio in his place. Drift!"

"No sheriffin' for mine, thanks. Contracting is my line. Subcontracting!"

"So long, boys! You know what I'd like to say. You gave me a square deal, you three chaps," said Foy. "Get word to Stella as soon as ever you can. She thinks I'm a prisoner, you know. You know what I want to say there, Pringle—tell her for me. . . . Say! Why don't you all go in now? You boys all know that Stella's engaged to me, don't you? What's the good of keeping her in suspense? Go on to the ranch, right away."

"I told you your head wasn't working just right," jeered Nueces. "We want to give you a good start. They'll be after you again, and you're in no fix to do any hard riding. But one of us will go. Breslin, you go."

"Too late," observed Anastacio quietly. There is Miss Vorhis now, with her father. They're climbing to the Gap. Go on, Foy."

"They've got a led horse," said Nueces as Stella and the Major came to the highest point of the Gap. "Who's that for? Chris? But they couldn't know about Chris. And how did they get here so quick? Don't seem like they've had hardly time."

Stella dismounted; she pressed on up the hill to meet her lover. The first sunshafts struck into the Gap, lit up the narrow walls with red glory.

Magic Casements! thought Pringle.

"Watch Foy get over the ground!" said Anastacio. "He'll break his neck before he gets down. I don't blame him. He's nearly down. Look the other way, boys!"

They looked the other way, and there were none to see that meeting. Unless, perhaps, the gods looked down from high Olympus—the poor immortals—and turned away, disconsolate, to the cheerless fields of asphodel.[54]

"But they're not going away," said Breslin after a suitable interval.

"They're waiting; and the Major's waving his hat at us."

"I'll go see what they want," said Anastacio.

In a few minutes he was back, rather breathless and extremely agitated in appearance.

"Well? Spill it!" said Nueces. "Get your breath first. What's the trouble?"

---

54 An underworld region in Greek mythology.

"Applegate's dead. Joe Espalin, I arrest you for the murder of Richard Marr! Applegate confessed!"

"He lied! He lied!" screamed Espalin. "I was with Ben till daylight, at the monte game; they all tell you. The sheriff he try to make me keel heem—he try to buy me to do eet—he keel Dick Marr heemself!"

"That's right!" spoke Creagan, suddenly white and haggard. His voice was a cringing whine; his eyes groveled. "Marr was at Lisner's house. We all went over there after the fight. Lisner waked Marr up—he'd been tryin' to egg Marr on to kill Foy all day, but Marr was too drunk. He was sobering up when we waked him. Lisner tried to rib him up to go after Foy and waylay him—told him he had been threatening Foy's life while he was drunk, and that Foy'd kill him if he didn't get Foy first. Dick said he wouldn't do it—he'd go along to help arrest Foy, but that's all he'd do. The sheriff and Joe went out together for a powwow. The sheriff came back alone, black as thunder—him and Dick rode off together—"

The sheriff sprang to his feet, his heavy face bloated and blotched with terror.

"He cursed me; he tried to pull his gun!" he wailed. His eyes protruded, glaring; one hand clutched at his throat, the other spread out before him as he tottered, stumbling. "Oh, my God!" he sobbed.

"That will do nicely," said Anastacio. "You're guilty as hell! I'll put your own handcuffs on you. Oddly enough, the law provides that when it is necessary to arrest the sheriff the duty falls to the coroner. It is very appropriate. You must pardon me, Mr. Lisner, if I seem unsympathetic. Dick Marr was your friend! And you have not been entirely fair with Foy, I fear. . . . Creagan, we'll hold you and Joe for complicity and for conspiracy in Foy's case. We'll arrest Applegate, too, when we get to camp. He'll be awfully vexed."

"What!" shrieked the sheriff, raising his manacled hands. "Liar! Murderer!"

"So Applegate's not dead? Well, I'm just as well pleased," said Pringle.

"Not even hurt badly. I was after the Man Lower Down. What the Major told me was that the Barelas were at the ranch—more than enough to hold Lisner's crowd down. They come at daylight. I was expecting that, and waiting. As I told you, that's the best thing I do—waiting."

"But how did you know?" demanded Breslin, puzzled.

"I didn't know, for sure. I had a hunch and I played it. So I killed poor Applegate—temporarily. It worked out just right and nothing to carry."

"One of the mainest matters with the widely-known world," said Pringle wearily, "is that people won't play their hunches. They haven't spunk enough to believe what they know. Let me spell it out for you in words of two cylinders, Breslin: You saw that I knew Creagan and Applegate, while they positively refused to know me at any price; you heard the sheriff deny that I was at the Gadsden House before I'd claimed anything of the sort. Of course you didn't know anything about the fight at the Gadsden House, but that was enough to show you something wasn't right, just the same. You had all the material to build a nice plump hunch. It all went over your head. You put me in mind of the lightning bug:

> The lightning bug is brilliant,
> But it hasn't any mind;
> It wanders through creation
> With its headlight on behind.[55]

"Come on—let's move. I'm fair dead for sleep."

"Just a minute!" said Anastacio. "I want to call your attention to the big dust off in the north. I've been watching it half an hour. That dust, if I'm not mistaken, is the Bar Cross coming; they've heard the news!"

"So, Mr. Lisner, you hadn't a chance to get by with it," said Pringle slowly and thoughtfully. "If I hadn't balked you, the Barelas stood ready; if the Barelas failed, yonder big dust was on the way; half your own posse would have turned on you for half a guess at the truth. It's a real nice little world—and it hates a lie. A good many people lay their fine-drawn plans, but they mostly don't come off! Men are but dust, they tell us. Magnificent dust! This nice little old world of ours, in the long run, is going right. You

55 A children's rhyme, authorship unknown.

can't beat the Game! Once, yes—or twice—not in the long run. The Percentage is all against you. You can't beat the Game!"

"It's up to you, Sheriff," said Anastacio briskly. "I can turn you over to the Bar Cross outfit and they'll hang you now; or I can turn you over to the Barelas and you will be hung later. Dick Marr was your friend! Take your choice. You go on down, Pringle, while the sheriff is looking over the relative advantages of the two propositions. I think Miss Vorhis may have something to say to you."

She came to meet him; Foy and the Major waited by the horses. "John!" she said. "Faithful John!" She sought his hands.

"There now, honey—don't take on so! Don't! It's all right! You know what the poet says:

Cast your bread upon the waters
And you may live to say:
"Oh, how I wish I had the crust
That once I threw away!"[56]

Her throat was pulsing swiftly; her eyes were brimming with tears, bruised for lost sleep.

"Dearest and kindest friend! When I think what you have done for me—that you faced shame worse than death—guarded by unprovable honor—John! John!"

"Why, you mustn't, honey—you mustn't do that! Why, Stella, you're crying—for me! You mustn't do that, Little Next Door!"

"If you had been killed, taking Chris—or after you gave him up—no one but me would have ever believed but that you meant it."

"But you believed, Stella?"

"Oh, I knew! I knew!"

"Even when you first heard of it?"

---

56 Rhodes' parody of Ecclesiastes 11:1: "Cast your bread upon the waters and you will find it after many days."

"I never doubted you—not one instant! I knew what you meant to do. You knew I loved him. The led horse was for you. I thought Chris would be gone. Why, John Wesley, I have known you all my life! You couldn't do that! You couldn't! Oh, kiss me, kiss me—faithful John!"

But he bent and kissed her hands—lest, looking into his eyes, she should read in the book of his life one long, long chapter—that bore her name.

Biographical Notes

Eugene Manlove Rhodes (1869–1934) lived and worked on southern New Mexico cattle ranches as a teenager and later owned his own ranch in Doña Ana County. He began his professional writing career in 1896 and became a regular contributor of western fiction to *Out West* magazine in 1902 and the *Saturday Evening Post* in 1907. In all, he published seven books and about a hundred stories set in New Mexico during the late-nineteenth and early-twentieth century. After his death, Rhodes was interred at his request at Rhodes Pass in the San Andrés mountains near his old ranch.

Gary Scharnhorst is Distinguished Professor Emeritus of English at the University of New Mexico. The author or editor of more than sixty scholarly books, he is a former chair of the American Literature Section of the Modern Language Association and a former president of the Western Literature Association.

www.ingramcontent.com/pod-product-compliance
Lightning Source LLC
LaVergne TN
LVHW051004080826
845145LV00009B/2441

* 9 7 8 0 8 2 6 3 6 9 5 7 4 *